PsiScouts #1:

At Risk

Don Sakers &
Phil Meade

PSI SCOUTS #1: AT RISK
copyright © 2003, Speed-of-C Productions

Published by
    Speed-of-C Productions
    811 Camp Meade Rd
    Linthicum, MD 21090-3030

ISBN: 978-1-9347-5421-4
August 2019

Dedicated To:

Eando Binder, John W. Campbell, Jr.,
Edmond Hamilton, Paul Levitz,
Jim Shooter, Jerry Siegel,
E.E. "Doc" Smith, Mort Weisinger,
Jack Williamson,
and all the rest of
the original Scouts.

Part One:

*The Case of the
Mega-Billionaire Target*

April AD 2574

The cargo robot was right on his heels. Royd Kar scrambled up a stack of crates, hoping the 'bot couldn't follow. The slick duraplast surface of the crates didn't offer much purchase, and the 'bot didn't look like a climber.

He was right—the robot stopped, whirring and clicking, at the foot of the stack. One long, jointed manipulator arm reached upward, touching Royd's right foot; he kicked it away and pulled himself to the top crate.

There, five meters up, Royd thumbed his nose at the 'bot. Then, curious, he stretched out on his stomach and watched the machine. What would it do?

After a few minutes the 'bot seemed to lose interest. It rolled away, feelers waving in the air before it. Perhaps, Royd reflected, it had thought he was loose cargo and only wanted to secure him. After he'd stopped moving, the dimwitted thing concluded that he was safely stowed.

Great, he thought. Am I supposed to stay here for three days without moving?

Stowing away aboard the *Terran Queen* had seemed such a good idea when Royd had first thought of it, a week ago and safe home on Taarla. Now, after thirty hours with only catnaps and with hunger gnawing at his stomach, he began to wonder if he'd made a mistake.

Maybe, Royd thought as he huddled down on his perch, maybe he should turn himself in. After all, what would the authorities do to the 14-year-old runaway? Even though he'd passed his preliminary adulthood tests, and was considered a full citizen on Taarla, surely Earth cops wouldn't be too harsh on a kid?

But would they let him stay on Earth? Or even get off the ship there? Hardly likely. They'd bundle him up and ship him back to his parents. Back to the leaky, one-room shack they called home. Back to the government dole that paid three people only enough for one, back to the mines that were the only work opportunity on the whole burnt-out cinder of a planet.

Royd's family hadn't always been poor. He had dim memories of new clothes and a spacious home with a beautiful garden, of household robots and tri-di and enough to eat every day. His father had been an ironball champ, famous throughout the sector; his mother had parlayed Papa's earnings into a winning portfolio that got her a powerful position at a major investment firm.

But then Papa was injured, and the Crash turned all Mama's stocks and bonds into meaningless bits in worthless computers. Royd hadn't known at the time that the Depression affected everyone in the world; for years he'd thought it was his fault that the family had left their wonderful home and moved into a succession of shacks, each worse than the one before.

Papa, injured, couldn't work in the mines—and Mama, a native Earthwoman, wasn't qualified. So the family went on the dole, and Royd sat with his Papa in the town square as the old man shook a begging bowl at passing strangers.

Royd blinked back hot tears and wiped his nose with the back of his hand. No, he couldn't turn himself in; going back home would be more than defeat, more than humiliation. It would be the end of all his dreams. Six days in the mines had convinced him that he wouldn't last a year without turning into the same kind of dull-witted, prematurely-aged drone who staffed the work crews around him.

No, Royd's only hope—his *family's* only hope—was for him to get off-planet, find some place where honest work was available and he could make enough to send some home. Royd's dream was to go to Earth and get a good job, work hard, and eventually bring Papa and Mama to live with him. For a moment he was lost in the vision of their faces suffused with delight when the one-way ticket to Earth arrived.

Royd sniffed and shook his head. Unless he got to Earth, he could kiss the rest of his dream goodbye. Stowing away had been the only way to get offplanet, and he'd jumped at his chance when the *Terran Queen* set down. But he hadn't planned for a three-day journey through hyperspace. The vast cargo hold, fortunately, had a rest room facility—but there was no food, and now with the cargo 'bot after him he didn't dare go in search of any. For that matter, he didn't dare use the bathroom, either.

Royd felt movement behind him and turned sharply. Another robot, a meter-high spiderlike affair, was creeping toward him across piled boxes, its eight legs moving gingerly from perch to perch. Sensors waved before it like antennae, and a pair of strong waldoes opened and closed with the repeated click of metal against metal.

"Damn it," he shouted, "What do I have to do around here? Can't you give me a fair chance?" The larger 'bot had obviously not lost interest in Royd; it had simply gone off to call this climber.

For the barest instant, Royd considered letting the 'bot grab him, no matter what the Earth police would do. Then he clenched his fists and set his jaw. "You're not going to get me without a fight," he said to the approaching monstrosity.

Royd closed his eyes and raised his hands, spreading his fingers. The robot's skin was made of duraplast, but there were steel parts within—Royd could feel the metal skeleton, the battery, the tangle of wires inside the robot....

Taarla was an unstable world whose magnetic field was in constant flux, a world where even the smallest predators could generate electrical charges that put Earth's electric eel to shame. The early colonists had been genetically engineered for sensitivity to magnetic fields; some few even gained a rudimentary psi ability to manipulate the lines of magnetic flux.

Over the centuries, these magnetic talents served Taarla's people well. Following invisible patterns, the people located the purest veins of precious metals and rare earths; the vast fortunes lost in the Crash had all grown from the early mines.

Royd had a Taarlan's sense of magnetic fields, but he had something else, inherited from his father: when it suited him, Royd could gather those intangible magnetic lines and play them as a puppeteer plays his strings. In childhood, he had played with balls and rods and sheets of steel the way other children played with balloons and sticks and paper. Before the Crash ruined everything, Royd had hoped to become an ironball player like Papa, perhaps even greater.

Hungry, angry, and afraid, Royd reached out to the approaching 'bot…and pulled.

The 'bot hung for an instant, its splayed legs frantically twitching. Then, helpless, it rocketed past Royd and shot across the cargo hold. The poor thing was still gaining speed when it hit the far wall with a sickening screech, then plummeted to become an ungainly, quivering lump on the deck below.

Now he'd done it. The broken robot would surely bring one of the crew to investigate. And if they came, they would find Royd.

He shrugged. So now there was nothing to lose.

Grinning, Royd scrambled down the stack of boxes and dropped to the deck. He strode confidently to the nearest hatchway. Beyond it were the passenger levels—and somewhere in them, there was food, and showers, and soft beds with fresh white sheets.

The hatch was sealed with a simple magnetic lock. Royd gestured, the hatch opened, and he stepped through.

❖

It didn't take Royd long to find food.

The *Terran Queen* kept Earth Standard Time, so it was the middle of the evening when Royd stepped out of the cargo hold. He walked down the spotless white corridor, glancing back over his shoulder every few seconds, until he came to a computer display, bright lines in the corridor wall.

Royd paused before the display, trying to locate the switch that would activate it.

"*Breep*. May I help you?"

Royd stepped back in surprise. The only talking 'puters he'd heard for years were the ones at the dole office. Those machines were hardly so well-mannered, and they would never offer to help.

"Do you require assistance?" the 'puter asked again.

"Yes. I'm starved. Where can I get something to eat?"

"There are sixty-three food service points currently in operation. Would you care to state more specific requirements?"

"Whatever's closest," Royd answered over a distinct growling from his stomach.

"Buffet supper is being served in Refectory C-3, open to all passengers. The menu includes—"

"Sounds cosmic. How do I get there?"

A blinking green light appeared on the wall, then moved to Royd's left. "Follow the directional light."

"Oh. Okay. Thanks."

Refectory C-3 was a good-sized dining room that reminded Royd of the cafeteria in elementary school. Two dozen passengers filled perhaps half the tables. At the front of the room, a hologram of a popular Earth band performed their latest music; but Royd made a beeline for the generously-stacked tables of food in the back.

He resisted the temptation to start cramming food into his mouth, and instead calmly snagged a plate and stepped into line. If the other passengers noticed his disheveled clothes or the rather stale scent that accompanied them, none mentioned it. The robot attendants at the buffet were equally silent.

When his plate was completely full, a tower of assorted hot and cold delicacies that swayed alarmingly with his every step, Royd found an isolated table and took a seat. The meal was the best he'd ever tasted, and he didn't stop until his plate was totally clear.

The sight of the dessert cart, two full meters of cakes and pies and puddings and ices, convinced him to leave the table. When he returned, someone else was waiting for him.

She was a tall, gangly girl about his own age, with bright red hair and a homely face just losing its freckles. Her dark green jumpsuit was clean but rumpled, her hair cut in a short, casual style.

She thrust out her hand. "I'm Gael Rimma."

Putting down his desserts, Royd shook her hand. "Royd Kar," he said. Then, sitting, he gestured to his food. "Uh, do you mind if I…?"

"Go right ahead." Gael leaned back and waited until Royd had a bite in his mouth, then said, "I haven't seen you on the ship before."

Royd swallowed. "I…er…got on at Taarla."

Gael's eyes narrowed. "You weren't at the new passengers reception. I would have noticed." She put her elbows on the table and propped her chin up on her hands. "There are three other teenagers aboard, plus two toddlers and one baby. I pay attention to things like that."

"Yeah, well, I kinda stay to myself a lot," Royd answered, hoping she would take the broad hint and leave him alone.

Gael tossed her head. "The other three teeners are here with parents. I'm alone."

"Oh?" It was difficult to stay polite while wolfing down cherry pie, but Royd did his best.

"Yes. I come from Wargal. I'm going to Earth to try and find my older brother."

"Your brother's on Earth?" What next, the chocolate cake or the pudding? Both, Royd decided, spooning pudding atop his cake.

"No. I don't know where he is." She dipped a finger in Royd's pudding and brought it to her mouth. "Dwin left home a year ago, without telling anyone where he was going. However, we decided Earth would be a good place to start the search. The Earth Police have resources and connections throughout the Myriad Worlds and beyond."

"So your family sent you out alone to find this brother?" Royd couldn't hide his skepticism.

"Of course not. My Pater is a very practical man; he would never have come up with such an idea on his own. My twin brother Alywin and I made the decision; after that, it was merely a matter of convincing the Pater to go along with us." She lowered her eyes. "We are very good at convincing the Pater."

"Wow, you must be rich." Royd left out the rest of his thought—the part about "spoiled rotten."

Gael laughed. "Rich? Hardly! But we have a little money." She frowned. "Haven't you heard of The Electrical Twins?"

"What are they, a singing group?"

Gael shook her head. "Child, where have they been keeping you? Watch." She held her hand up, thumb and forefinger just a centimeter apart.

Without warning, a bright spark leapt across the gap, accompanied by a loud crack. Royd, startled, pulled back.

Half the people in the room turned to look; Gael gave an exaggerated shrug and they all went back to their meals. "Don't worry," she said, "I have it completely under control."

"How did you do that?"

"It's a psi power. Like I said: Alywin and me, we're The Electrical Twins. Masters of the mysterious forces of static- and bio-electricity. The Wonders of Wargal. Just two credits a ticket. We performed everywhere."

"Not on Taarla, I guess." Royd leaned closer. "You know, that's pretty cosmic. Have you always been able to do that?"

"That's what the doctors say. They say the power is probably latent in our whole family. But our abilities didn't manifest themselves until two years ago." She stared into Royd's eyes. "The story's been on all the channels. Are you sure you haven't heard it?"

Forgotten ice cream was puddling into soup on Royd's plate. "Just go ahead and tell it, okay?"

"All right. The three of us—Dwin, Alywin, and I—were on a camping trip with our sitter. At least, we were supposed to go camping. Anyway, our boat went down on Roblak—that's Wargal's largest moon." Now that she was actually into her tale, Gael seemed reluctant to continue. "Nitrogen/Carbon dioxide atmosphere, lots of electrical storms. Anyway, after we sat for a while, Dwin had this wonderful idea that we could run up a spike and use lightning to recharge our batteries and send a message for help."

"Did it work?"

"About as well as any of Dwin's other ideas. The lightning strikes blasted our boat and killed the sitter right off. Alywin was burned and Dwin got knocked senseless. But apparently our latent psi powers came out and protected us."

"That's horrible."

"Yeah, I guess so. Turns out that a science satellite caught all the activity and notified the cops. They rescued us before our air ran out. Then we went on the road, and then Dwin ran away, and here I am." She spread her hands. "So you're a stowaway, eh?"

Royd felt like she'd just zapped him with her electrical powers. "Wh-what makes you say something like that?"

"I told you, I pay attention to things." She ticked off points on her fingers. "You're not exactly dressed like a passenger, you know. If you'd bought a ticket, you wouldn't talk about how rich I must be to afford one of my own. The ship's newsletter yesterday did a whole writeup on The Electrical Twins, but you hadn't heard of us. And you eat like you haven't seen food in three weeks."

Royd looked down at the remains of his desserts, then back at Gael. "It's only been two days, actually," he admitted.

"Why don't you tell me about it?"

Almost in spite of himself, Royd told her his sad story—the mines, his determination to find work on Earth, the cargo 'bots that had chased him, everything. When he finished, he rested his chin in his hands and sighed deeply. "So now I guess you'll turn me in, right?"

"Wrong. Now I'm going to take you back to my cabin and put you to bed. Then while you're sleeping I'll get on the hyperwave to home. By the time you wake up, you'll have a ticket, fair and square."

"I can't let you do that."

She stood up. She was almost as tall as Royd, and looked twice as tough. "You stupid boy, how do you think you're going to stop me?" Her glare softened. "The Pater has a lot of friends, and he loves doing things for me. So don't worry about it. Besides, you're a psionic like me. Us freaks have to stick together, nyet?"

Royd gave a weak smile. "All right. Thank you. I'll pay you back, really I will."

"Fine." She took his hand and pulled him to his feet. "Now let's get you settled. If I'm going to sweet-talk the Pater, I have to practice being nice."

❖

A good night's sleep and a tasty breakfast improved Royd's outlook on life. Of course, the trip ticket Gael handed him also lifted his spirits considerably.

Royd moved into the cabin next to Gael. The ship's steward, a handsome man in his thirties (who didn't seem the least bit surprised to have picked up a new passenger thirty lightyears from the nearest inhabited planet), found Royd some new clothes: a pale grey pair of slacks, a few pastel tunics, and a dark blue jumpsuit with the *Terran Queen* logo on the left sleeve and his name stitched on the front.

For the next two days, Royd spent every waking moment with Gael. There were a thousand things to do on the *Terran Queen*, and the crewmembers were only too happy to answer questions and give tours. Sometimes the other teeners joined them on these expeditions, but mostly it was just Gael, Royd, and the ever-present, ever-helpful ship's computer.

Royd was almost sorry to see the Terra System draw close. When he went to sleep for the last time on shipboard, he actually had to blink back a few self-pitying tears.

At three in the morning, six hours out from Earth, Royd sat suddenly upright in the dark, listening to the steady hum of the air recyclers. Something had changed. Something in the ship's air, or artificial gravity, or in the odd mixture of background noises, or….

Yes, that was it! *Terran Queen's* magnetic field, which had been rock-steady since leaving Taarla, had…shifted.

Just as the creak of a loose floorboard at home would instantly alert him that someone was up and about; just as the rush of water over his skin would tell him that someone had dived into the swimming hole with him—so this pulsing change in the lines of magnetic flux told him that somewhere on board, something was out of place.

Like a spider, following quivering strands to a thrashing fly trapped in her web, Royd held still, finding the direction of this magnetic anomaly.

Aft. Toward the cargo holds…and the engines!

He pulled on his jumpsuit, padded out into the hall, and tapped on Gael's door. She opened it at once.

"You felt it too?" Gael clutched a yellow bathrobe around her shoulders. Her feet were bare.

Royd nodded. "I can still feel it. It's off that way." He pointed. "Wait a minute, you're not sensitive to magnetic fields."

"But I *do* feel electrical potentials. And this one nearly took my head off. It was like a great big lightning bolt hitting next door." She closed her eyes and frowned. "It feels like there's another one building up now."

"Maybe it's something to do with approaching Earth," Royd suggested. "Or dropping out of hyperdrive."

Gael shook her head. "De' Purna said they wouldn't even touch the engines until an hour before approach. I think something's wrong—and we ought to tell somebody."

"What do you mean? Call the Captain and say, excuse me, Ma'am, we think there's something wrong with your ship?"

Gael stood with her hands on her hips. "Well then, what do you suggest?"

Royd glanced aft down the corridor. "Let's take a look. It might be something simple, you know, magnetic lockdowns in the cargo bay or such. Then if we can't figure out where the distortion is coming from, we'll notify the crew. How does that sound?"

"Okay, I guess." She held up a finger. "Wait here while I put on some clothes."

❖

The thrumming magnetic distortion led them to the threshold of the engine room door. That door was closed and sealed, but Royd's magnetic abilities made short work of opening it.

He half-expected someone to stop them, but the large room was empty except for the massive graviton and stardrive engines that drove the ship, the antimatter reactor that powered them, and the display consoles that controlled both. Narrow catwalks threaded between hulking machinery, the air around them live with the sensation of enormous power held in perfect control, tremendous forces balanced against one another.

"We shouldn't be here," Royd whispered.

"I know," Gael answered, "But it's too late to turn back now. We might as well find the distortion."

Forward...left...and there it was. The magnetic distortion was invisible, existing deep inside the engine, but Royd felt it clearly through the grey metal of the engine's containment housing. "Right there," he said, pointing.

The Chief Engineer had opened an inspection hatch to show them the interior of one of the mighty engines—Royd remembered that the containment housing was ten centimeters of solid impervium, enough to stop an atomic blaster. Yet here the housing was cracked and visibly scorched.

Unconsciously Royd reached forward, following the pull of the hidden distortion. Gael knocked his hand aside.

"Watch it!" She pulled Royd back, stepping in front of him. "It's going to—"

With a loud crackle, eye-searing electrical bolts leapt from the damaged housing. Royd felt his hair stand on end and fell back—but Gael stood her ground. For an instant she was outlined in light, as electricity danced around her. Then the discharge ended, and she turned back to Royd with a smile. "Sorry."

"Hey, don't worry about it. You saved my life." The magnetic distortion lurched, then started getting larger, more powerful. "I don't think this is a harmless side effect," he said.

"No. We'd better go get someone right away."

Royd frowned. "Gael, it feels like it's spreading. I don't think leaving is such a good idea."

Her eyes were wide. "Can you do anything?"

"I'll try." Royd closed his eyes, concentrating on the insubstantial lines of magnetic flux. He felt his way around the distortion, trying to get a feel for its shape and properties.

The ship was embedded in a strong, solid magnetic bubble —and this distortion was like a ragged hole in the bubble. A hole that was expanding, growing less stable with each passing second.

What if the bubble popped? Would the resulting explosion destroy the ship—or just drop them out of hyperdrive and strand them a hundred billion kilometers away from the nearest planet?

He didn't want to find out.

Moving quickly and surely, Royd extended his own field, gathered the edges of that hole, and…tugged. There was resistance, then he felt the hole stabilize. As long as he could hold on, it would get no larger.

"I…think…I have it," he grunted. "But I don't know…how long I can…hold it." Right now, stabilizing the distortion was about as strenuous as lifting his baby brother. But he could feel deeper and stronger forces stirring within the engine. Soon, he knew, he would tire….

"What the hell is going on here?" Chief Engineer Purna, a meter and a half of smoldering fury, bore down on the two kids, followed by half a dozen of the crew. Her expression made it clear that someone was about to get chewed out.

Royd started to explain. "There's a tear in the magnetic field—"

"What have you kids done to my engines? Get away from there before you make things worse." Purna moved toward Royd.

He stayed where he was. He had his own magnetic field braced against the ship's hull; if he moved, he might lose control. "De' Purna, you have to listen."

"Kid, you don't have any idea what you're—"

Gael held her hands before her, half a meter apart, and lightning danced between them. Purna came to a skidding halt.

"Thank you," Gael said. "You're right, Royd and I *don't* know what we're doing. But before we stop doing it, you'd better take a look at the engine's magnetic field."

One of the crew was already at a console. After a moment, he lifted a pale face to Purna. "There's a rupture in the field. Right now it's stabilized—I don't know how. But if it goes, it'll tear the whole engine apart."

Purna's face went from rage to fear, then settled into an expression of disbelief. "All right, kid, what are you doing?"

"I'm a magnetokinetic. I've got ahold of the rupture and I'm trying to hold it closed."

"Like the boy with his finger in the dike," the crewman said. "If he lets go…."

"I know," Purna answered. "Listen, uh…."

"Royd," he supplied.

"Thanks. Listen, Royd, how much longer can you hold that rupture?"

"I don't know. When I grabbed it, I wasn't thinking in terms of holding it for long. I just grabbed." He frowned. "I've never done anything like this before."

"All right. I have to report to the Captain. Can you keep this steady for, oh, five minutes?"

"Sure." The magnetic field lurched, struggling to tear itself free of his control. He steadied it…but the effort was greater than the first time. "I hope," he added.

"Do your best." Purna retreated, leaving her crew gaping at Royd and Gael.

❖

Half an hour later, the Captain made an announcement to the whole ship. Royd, struggling to hold the magnetic rupture steady, listened with half an ear to the words booming through the engine room.

"Ladies and gentlemen, I am sorry to inform you that there will be a sudden change in our schedule. We have developed some minor engine trouble that will make it necessary for the *Terran Queen* to lay over at the Himalia Shipyards around Jupiter."

Gael grunted. "`Minor engine trouble.' Ha!"

Royd's right leg was starting to cramp; he shifted his weight carefully. "The Captain just doesn't want anyone to panic." He knew that the situation was a bit more grave than the Captain let on. At that moment, a hyperspace tug was on its way to tow the *Terran Queen* to Himalia; as soon as it arrived, the Engineering crew would shut down the malfunctioning engine.

Until then, Royd was their only hope.

"Passengers for Earth will transfer to the regularly-scheduled Ganymede shuttle; passengers to Runtalex and beyond will be routed to Deimos and will travel on our sister ship, the *Martian Queen*. All luggage and cargo will be automatically transferred. We apologize for any inconvenience."

"Well, that's mighty nice to hear," Gael said. She stepped into position next to Royd. "Hold on, it's going to discharge again. Jobo, stand back."

Jobo—the short, stocky crewman who had stuck by Royd and Gael since the ordeal started—moved out of the way.

The routine was growing familiar now. The magnetic distortion triggered an electrical discharge every three to five minutes. As soon as Gael sensed a discharge coming, she moved into position to absorb it, while Royd braced himself to hold the field steady. The stresses were worst then.

Following the discharge, they had another period of relative calm while another built up.

Blue-white electricity leapt from the damaged engine to Gael's waiting hands. When it subsided, she shivered. "The charges are getting stronger," she observed.

Jobo glanced at an instrument in his hand. "Yup. The tug is on her way, but she won't get here for another half hour at least. Can you two hold out that long?"

Royd gave a wry smile. "We'll have to, won't we?"

Jobo shrugged. "We can do an emergency core dump in five minutes. And risk a pretty big explosion when the field destabilizes. If you can stand it, Chief Engineer would rather wait until we transfer the passengers to the tug."

Gael chuckled. "We're passengers too, you know."

Jobo waved to another crewmember. "Lenka, toss me your cap!" Lenka threw her dark blue cap; Jobo snagged it and set it on Gael's head. Then he took off his own cap and plopped it backwards atop Royd's brown curls. "Not any more, you aren't."

❖

By the time the last passenger moved to the tug, the engine room was getting distinctly crowded. Every engineer, in addition to any other crewmembers who felt involved, crammed into the catwalk to watch Royd and Gael.

Gael seemed to be right in her element, happy and full of energy, but Royd was getting tired of the whole performance. His arms and shoulders ached, his throat was dry, and his head throbbed in time with the magnetic distortion.

The Captain was the last to arrive. Standing tall in her dress uniform, she strode to the Chief Engineer, who saluted smartly. "What's the situation, Chief?"

"Holding steady, Ma'am."

The Captain nodded. "The passengers are safe. I suggest you dismiss De' Rimma and De' Kar, and then shut down these bothersome engines."

From the corner of his eye, Royd caught Jobo turning his head to cover a snicker.

"Begging your pardon, Ma'am, but De' Rimma and De' Kar are the only things holding this engine together. I suggest —"

The distortion chose that moment to emit a searing discharge that left purple afterimages dancing across Royd's vision. Gael stumbled backward, and if Jobo hadn't steadied her she might have fallen to the floor.

"That's it," the Chief Engineer announced, moving in toward Royd and Gael. "Engineers, take your consoles. Cap'n, I'd appreciate it if you could move all the rest of these people out of the way." She faced Royd. "Son, we're going to have to collapse this field and damp the engines down to nothing. But if that hole moves while we're doing that, we'll have an uncontrolled reaction on our hands. I think you can hold the hole; what do you think?"

Royd took a deep breath. "I can do it."

"Right."

The Captain and the others were in full retreat, leaving only the engineering crew at their stations. Chief Engineer Purna called out their names, one at a time, and they answered, "Ready."

When the last one was accounted for, she put her hand on Royd's shoulder. "If you feel like you're losing control, yell `stop' and we'll freeze it right where it is. Okay?"

"Okay."

Gael touched his other shoulder. She was grinning like a fool. "You can do it, Royd."

"I hope so." He closed his eyes, feeling the distortion's flux like a wild animal struggling to escape his grasp. "All right, let's do it."

Chief Purna counted to three, then Royd was very busy. The distortion surged in his magnetic grip, bucked, and almost tore free. Around him he felt the ship's magnetic field collapsing, swirling like water down a drain.

Lightning flashed in the narrow space, battering Gael and leaving the smell of ozone in its wake. For an instant, gravity washed across them like waves quitting a shore. Royd grunted, and Chief Purna swore.

Hold…hold…keep holding… unconsciously, Royd felt the tip of his tongue creep out between his teeth.

He was aware of a distant shout—"I can't hold it, it's going exponential!"—and suddenly the distortion had twisted free, the entire ship's field was flapping about like a rapidly-deflating balloon….

Gael gripped his arm tightly. Fleetingly, Royd wondered how much she could sense of this magnetic chaos—surely it had some effect on local electrical fields? He swallowed hard, spread his magnetic reach as far as he could, and squeezed.

The effort was like wrapping his arms around an epileptic elephant. It was too much, the strain would tear him apart.

No, he thought. Those aren't my arms, and I'm not trying to surround anything. That kind of thinking isn't going to get me anywhere. I'm at the center of a magnetic field that reaches as far as I can think. Don't move around the opposing field; move with it. Through it. He tried to remember what his karate teacher had taught him. Breathe. Center.

There…yes…he had it now. More like swimming than wrestling. The field moved around and with him, yielded to his motion, followed his direction. It shrunk, and in shrinking it became tamer, less resistant. Smaller, more manageable, something that he could contain within his arms, between his hands, finally between finger and thumb—and then, miraculously, the field was gone, shut down, and Royd fell back against the bulkhead with relief.

Gael smiled and gripped his shoulder. "You did it, Royd! Congratulations."

❖

The Captain asked to see Royd and Gael once they were aboard the tug. She met them in a small anteroom off the tug's bridge; there was barely room for the three of them to stand.

She briskly shook hands with each of them. "De' Kar, De' Rimma, I must thank you for what you did today. If it hadn't been for your resourcefulness and your…er…unusual talents, everyone on the ship might have been killed. Not to mention the loss of a ship worth several million credits. The company is very grateful to you."

Royd looked away, embarrassed.

"De' Kar, the purser tells me that there were certain, uh, irregularities in your ticket for this voyage."

"I can explain," Royd began.

"Never mind, lad. It's all been straightened out. I instructed the purser to refund both of your tickets." The Captain reached into her pocket and took out two datacards. "The Company has also authorized me to give you these cards: they're good for unlimited passage on any ship the Company flies."

"Anywhere?" Royd echoed.

"As many times as we want?" Gael added.

The Captain smiled. "Yes. You've earned those passes; enjoy them." She nodded. "Now if you'll excuse me, I have to make sure these tug pilots don't damage my ship."

❖

The tug came out of hyperdrive twelve million kilometers from Jupiter, carrying the *Terran Queen* behind it like an ant dragging a grasshopper. From the tug's observation lounge, Royd and Gael had a beautiful view of Jupiter. The giant planet hung warm and orange against star-peppered black. Bands and whorls of pastel reds, yellows, and browns, frozen by immense size and distance, chased one another around the flattened globe.

Jobo, the engineer, pointed and said, "Look, there's the shuttle." A small speck of light blossomed into the swept-wing form of the Ganymede/Earth shuttle, an intricate toy that swelled as the two ships matched orbits.

Soon the shuttle loomed so large that it eclipsed Jupiter, and Royd thought he could see the excited faces of passengers gazing out of their viewports as they enjoyed this unexpected diversion.

"Attention passengers for Earth," the Purser's voice boomed. "Please follow the glowing arrows to Access Port Five for connection to the Earth shuttle. Your luggage will be automatically transferred, and will be waiting for you when you arrive in New York. Once again, we apologize for the inconvenience you have suffered."

"Come on." Gael grabbed Royd's arm and pulled him along. "We want to get good seats."

About twenty passengers were transferring to the Earth shuttle. Gael and Royd were at the front of the line. After a series of miscellaneous clanks and thumps, the heavy airlock door slid ponderously aside, and Gael scrambled forward into the shuttle.

A steward met them with a smile. "You're De' Rimma and De' Kar? I'm afraid that we had to stick you in First Class; I hope you don't mind?"

Gael nodded. "That will be fine."

The First Class section was divided into a series of curtained alcoves, each holding four luxuriously-padded seats centered around a small table, and a large wallscreen that showed the view outside so convincingly that Royd thought it was a window.

Two of the seats in the alcove that the steward took them to was occupied—by a fat, elderly woman and a thin, pale, teenage girl. As they took their seats, the old woman stuck out a huge hand. "Hello. I'm Colleen Artveldt," she boomed. "Very pleased to meet you. Sit down, sit down!"

Gael looked surprised as she shook the woman's hand. "*The* Colleen Artveldt?" she asked.

She laughed. "Are there that many, my dear? Yes, I'm the one."

When Royd looked puzzled, Gael said to him, "De' Artveldt is one of the richest people in the Galaxy. She's worth megabillions." She turned to Artveldt. "I'm Gael Rimma. And this is my friend Royd Kar."

Royd shook the woman's hand. One of the richest people in the Galaxy? Could it be true? Blushing, he wondered how he could go about asking Artveldt for a job.

Gael gestured from the teenage girl to Artveldt. "And are you…?"

The girl turned toward Gael, her pale face passive and devoid of emotion. "No," she said in a monotone. "My name is Iris Krall. I am from Ceres."

For the first time, Royd noticed the girl's forehead tattoo, just a shade or two lighter than her skin and partly hidden by her dark hair: the Greek letter psi. The mark of a telepath.

And an accomplished one, if she were from Ceres, home of the Telepathic Institute and the most talented mindreaders in the Myriad Worlds.

Before Royd could inquire further, a bell-tone interrupted his thoughts. "Attention passengers, please fasten your seat belts in preparation for departure."

As soon as they were clear of the tug and the *Terran Queen*, De' Artveldt nodded and turned her attention to a portable terminal. "Business, you know," she said apologetically, burying herself in a maze of glowing figures, charts, and graphs that surrounded her in three-dimensional splendor.

Iris Krall sat back in her chair and closed her eyes, sitting perfectly rigid, and with a look on her face that said she had a terrible migraine.

Gael touched a control on the arm of her chair, and Royd saw the slight haze of a privacy field engulf their two chairs. "Colleen Artveldt!" she said. "Can you believe it?"

Royd nodded. "We were lucky to land in First Class."

Gael gave him a slightly condescending smile. "Oh, Royd, you are so naive. You don't think it was just luck, do you? The Purser on the *Terran Queen* did us another favor. The others are all stuck back in coach." She prodded Royd with an elbow and nodded in Artveldt's direction. "Say, you don't suppose her company is hiring?"

Royd grinned. "I'd love it. But I'm afraid to ask her. Besides, she's very busy. It doesn't look like she wants to talk with anyone right now."

"Yeah," Gael agreed, frowning. "And it doesn't look like she's having fun, either. Maybe you *don't* want to work for her outfit."

With a chuckle, Royd keyed the privacy field off, and watched the endless stars that drifted slowly across the wallscreen.

Shortly, a steward appeared with a large tray of food and drinks, which he arranged on the table. Artveldt shut down her displays, rubbed her hands together, and grinned. "Well, this looks like quite a spread." She smeared a cracker high with a sort of orange-brown mush and thrust it at Royd. "Vela-bird pate," she said proudly. "Have you ever tried it?"

"N-no," Royd croaked, staring cross-eyed at the cracker.

"Go ahead, it's delicious. And some for the young lady."

Taking a deep breath, Royd bit into the cracker. It was delicious.

Royd and Gael dug in, encouraged by Artveldt's enthusiasm and casual gluttony. Soon, even Iris Krall was tasting some of the treats.

"So," Artveldt said around a mouthful, "What brings you young people to Earth?"

"I'm searching for my lost brother," said Gael.

"And I'm searching for a job," said Royd.

"Hah!" Artveldt punched a code into her terminal and handed the small printout slip to Royd. "When you get settled on Earth, give a call to that number. Artveldt Enterprises can always use talented young people. I'm sure we'll be able to find you something."

"Th-thank you," Royd sputtered.

Artveldt dismissed him with a wave. "Nothing, nothing." She turned to Iris Krall. "And what about you, my lovely?"

"I have been assigned to the Earth Police as a detective-interrogator."

Artveldt frowned. "You don't sound as if you're looking forward to it."

Iris shrugged. "I accept my assignment from the Institute without complaint." She closed her eyes and settled back in her chair. "I am sorry. I am not accustomed to...so many minds. I must rest."

Artveldt grinned slyly and tucked another printout into Iris's hand. "Life is too short to spend it on a job you don't like," she said. "Hold onto that number, and if you can't stand being a detective-interrogator, give us a call."

She turned back to the food. "Now, who wants some Bernallian tiger-grapes?"

As he munched, Royd examined Iris Krall, trying to pretend he was merely looking at the wallscreen. She's pretty enough, he thought. Pity she's so...unfriendly. She might be fun if she opened up a little. Like Gael.

Royd was shocked when Iris opened her eyes and looked right at him. *If you were surrounded by the minds of a hundred strangers, perhaps you would have trouble opening up, as well.*

Her lips hadn't moved; Gael and Artveldt had not heard a thing.

Embarrassed, Royd looked away. Iris closed her eyes again and went back to her rest.

The steward returned and removed the food and drinks. Shortly afterward, an announcement came: "Attention passengers, please prepare for landing."

On the wallscreen, Earth swam into view, achingly blue-white against star-strewn darkness. A gibbous moon floated brilliant bone white beyond the planet's limb. Royd shivered; seeing Earth for real was so much more impressive than the same view in postcards and holos from vacationing friends. Here it was: Earth, fair Terra, home world of the Human species. The oldest relics of Taarla were only a hundredth the age of Earth's oldest ruins.

Entry into Earth's atmosphere was a very bumpy process. Gael enjoyed every jolt and jostle, bouncing excitedly—but Royd noticed that Iris kept her eyes screwed shut and was gripping the arms of her chair with white knuckles.

She's scared, he thought.

So are you, came an echo in his mind. He wasn't certain if the voice was Iris's, or his own.

The planet spun dizzily and clouds banked fast. He looked away from the wallscreen and tried to ignore Gael's delighted shouts; instead, he focussed on keeping his stomach under control.

I hate this, he thought.

So do I, came Iris's voice within his head. An unseen gesture brought his attention to Gael. *She is certainly enjoying it, though.* Tentatively, she continued, *She says we can try to share her sensations.*

You can do that?

He saw Iris give a slight nod. *I think so. A simple level one rapport. Let me try.*

Royd looked at the viewport and felt everything change. The landscape raced past, terribly canted, then lurched as the ship suddenly dived. A moment earlier Royd would have been clutching the arms of his chair and fighting nausea; now, he laughed.

There was nothing scary about this. It was…fun.

Royd was distantly aware of Iris and Gael sharing this miraculous transformation—but at the forefront of his mind, he was far more conscious of the experience itself: the buffeting of high-altitude winds, the exhilarating feeling of speed. He found himself wishing, just a little, that they would turn down the artificial gravity and let him feel a little of the ship's motion.

All too soon, the domes of New York were on the horizon, and the shuttle landed at Terraport.

As soon as the ship was motionless, the landing platform sunk, carrying the shuttle into a large underground hangar. Twenty-five meters down, the shuttle moved forward, and the landing platform rose again.

The wallscreen went blank, and a steward appeared. "Right this way, please."

De' Artveldt stood, motioning the teenagers to go before her. "You young people go first," she said. "I'll bring up the rear."

Royd didn't argue. He was very anxious to be off the shuttle, to touch Terran ground. And he knew, from the lingering trace of Iris's rapport, that the other two were equally anxious.

They stopped at the hatch, held up behind a tall, middle-aged man who had all the stewards busy trying to sort out a problem with some luggage he'd apparently brought aboard at the last minute.

Gael fumed at the delay, leaving the air smelling slightly of ozone. Royd peered past the tall man, struggling to get a glimpse of the promised land: Earth.

A short boarding ramp led down from the shuttle to a crowded slidewalk that curved away behind the ship, toward the distant terminal. The huge, vaulting cave of the underground hangar was festooned with ladders, stairways, ramps, and platforms; the ground level was a seething hive of activity. Cargo vehicles, robots, passengers, and official-garbed human dashed one way and another. Everything was brilliantly lit and impeccably clean, beautiful in its stark functionality.

The tall man, apparently satisfied, moved forward. Gael, with Royd and Iris in tow, pushed forward onto the ramp.

Iris was trembling, and Royd could feel her fright. Here in the port, and in the great city beyond, millions of minds beat out a soundless cacophony of unshielded thoughts and emotions. Even for a well-trained telepath like Iris, the effort of shielding her mind from those millions of others was almost overwhelming.

This, she thought to Royd in a quick aside, *Is why telepaths do not often come to Earth.*

Halfway down the ramp, as De' Artveldt stepped out of the shuttle, Iris suddenly froze, grabbing Royd and Gael by the arms.

Wha—?

Someone wants to kill De' Artveldt.

Who?

Royd started to scan the surroundings, but Iris spotted them first. *There!*

A man and woman in Terraport uniforms stood ten meters away, on the ground by the shuttle's nose. Both had their attention on Colleen Artveldt, and both held guns pointed straight at the billionaire. In backwash from Iris's mind, Royd felt their intense concentration and cold sense of purpose.

Through the telepathic rapport that linked the three teens, there was no need for discussion or decision, no time for words. There was only complete agreement, based more on geometry than on thought.

Royd, closer to the woman, cast out with magnetic tendrils; her weapon went spinning. At the same instant, Gael gestured and the man recoiled, quite literally struck by lightning.

There was room only for confusion, for the beginning of a scream, then the would-be assassins bolted, running toward the terminal.

"Stop them!" Gael shouted, and someone else called "Get those kids!" Iris stepped back, took a deep breath, and closed her eyes. Then she hurled forth a mental command.

STOP!

Only the barest whisper of that command brushed Royd, but that mere whisper locked all his muscles into immobility. The fleeing man and woman stopped so suddenly that both tumbled to the ground.

Come here. Iris, shaking with effort, gripped the rail tightly. The man and woman, moving like marionettes, stumbled toward her and halted on the tarmac below and before her.

There was a pause, then Iris announced to the open-mouthed spectators: "They were hired to kill De' Artveldt. They do not know who hired them." She opened her eyes and sought out a woman in the sleek blue-and-grey uniform of Terraport Security. "You had better arrest them now, I do not know how much longer I can keep them under control."

The Security officer moved to comply.

While the criminals were handcuffed and led away, Royd and Gael helped Iris to the foot of the ramp. De' Artveldt, right behind them, clapped them on the back. "Splendid piece of teamwork, children! Very splendid indeed. You saved my life."

"It was nothing," Royd said, blushing. But Gael grinned from ear to ear.

"Hey, that *was* pretty good, wasn't it?"

By this time they were surrounded by a crowd of net newshawks and holovision reporters, all jostling to reach Artveldt. A wall of people in business suits materialized between De' Artveldt and the reporters.

"De' Artveldt, why do you think these two tried to take your life?"

"Do you recognize them?"

"Does this have anything to do with the Crimson Circle?"

"Is there any connection to your recent divorce?"

De' Artveldt held up a hand, silencing one and all. Then she held out an arm to Royd, Gael, and Iris. "These young people are the heroes of the day, not me. It's their story you ought to be telling. Why don't you ask them some questions?"

That opened the floodgates. For the next half hour, the three teens were busy answering questions, posing for holograms, and re-creating their dramatic rescue.

When the press finally withdrew, De' Artveldt was long-gone; but a fortyish man in a well-tailored business suit was waiting for them. "I'm Stan Lovan," he said, shaking hands with each of them in turn, "De' Artveldt's personal secretary. Colleen had a pressing engagement, but she instructed me to wait for you and see that you're settled. You're to be her guests in her penthouse tonight, and then she wants to see you first thing tomorrow morning."

"Oh, we couldn't—" Royd began.

"Shut up, Royd," Gael interrupted. "We'd be delighted. What about you, Iris?"

She looked around. "I was supposed to be met by...."

De' Lovan smiled. "I took the liberty of notifying the Earth Police of De' Artveldt's schedule and wishes. I assured them that you will check in as soon as you are settled. They were satisfied."

Iris shrugged. "Then I am satisfied as well."

"Splendid," Lovan nodded. "I've made arrangements for your baggage. If you'll come with me, please?"

❖

Colleen Artveldt's luxury penthouse hung from the underside of the Manhattan dome a quarter-kilometer above Central Park. The gleaming spires of the ancient city spread out in all directions like a vast bed of crystalline mineral deposits in unearthly shapes and colors.

The furnishings were no less spectacular than the view. Murals, fine tapestries, and beautiful artworks were everywhere. The penthouse was run by a corps of 'bots so efficient that half the time, the teenagers' wishes were granted before they even asked.

Lovan made sure that they were settled, then left them alone, explaining that he would be back the next morning to pick them up for their appointment with De' Artveldt.

Gael quickly discovered that the penthouse could get the very newest holovideos, and started a popular new feature running in the center of the well-appointed living room. She threw herself down on the luxurious couch, net to a large bowl of popcorn, and said, "Ah, this is the life!"

Royd, smiling but feeling a little guilty, nibbled at the popcorn but said nothing. It was hard to be surrounded by such luxury, knowing that the folks back on Taarla were having to split another one-ration dinner.

Iris sat stiff and still, keeping her thoughts to herself.

"Say," Gael asked, "What do you suppose De' Artveldt wants with us tomorrow?"

Royd stretched, stifling a yawn. "She probably wants to thank us again."

Gael nodded. "You know, that was fun, wasn't it?"

"Yes," Royd answered, "Yes, I guess it was."

Even Iris had to agree.

❖

After her conference in New York, Colleen Artveldt had appointments in London, Cairo, and Mexico City. By the time she returned to Manhattan, the sun was going down and a few brave stars were peeking out between scattered clouds.

De' Artveldt strode into her private office, dropping bits of outerwear as she went. She shrugged into a bathrobe held by an obedient robot, tied it closed, and accepted a drink from the bar. Then, perched in front of the small table that was the only desk she ever used, she started issuing orders. Her large staff of human lackeys, attendants, and Vice Presidents scrambled to comply.

"Jen, I want to know everything about those three children. Where did they come from, why are they here, who are their families, where were they educated, what are their favorite colors and holovid stars? Full reports on my terminal in two hours."

"Right away, Chief."

"Bok'Choor, talk to the director of Artveldt Youth Services. I want a summary of everything she has on that matter of at-risk kids. Get me someone from the Earth Police. And wake up Legal, I want them to be part of this as well."

"It shall be done."

"It better be." She looked around, frowned. "Where the hell is Dori?"

"At home with her new baby," De' Lovan said softly.

"Of course she is. I knew that." De' Artveldt narrowed her eyes. "I assume we sent flowers?"

"Yes, Colleen. And champagne. And a brand-new bassinet. And a promise not to disturb her, even for Judgement Day."

"As it should be. So who's in charge of PR now?"

"That would be Jenthen."

"Good. I want a conference with her, in half an hour. And who's that geneticist who's been pushing those theories about the Jemalli Fever?"

"Isaac Mbouti. You want to talk to him, too?"

"Yes. As soon as possible." De' Artveldt folded her arms, then looked around at the eyes all upon her. "Well, what are you all waiting for? I'm not paying you by the hour. We have a long night ahead of us. Get to work!"

❖

Morning came clear and bright to New York City. Royd awoke to a wonderful view and the aromas of bacon and coffee. Blue silk pajamas, in his size and monogrammed with his initials, were waiting for him. He pulled them on, attended to his toilet, and went in search of the delicious smells.

He found them emanating from a well-laden table in the dining room, watched over by a polished chrome 'botler.

The room commanded a spectacular view to the east. Beyond the dome, Royd saw clouds of spaceships rising from Terraport on their morning runs.

Gael, in fiery red pajamas, sat before a half-finished stack of pancakes. "We were wondering when you'd get up."

"Have something to eat before it all gets cold." Iris wore basic black, embroidered in black; her plate held a modest assortment of fruits.

As Royd slid into his chair, the 'botler placed a warmed plate before him. Royd chose modestly from the bounty, although he did take a double portion of bacon.

"Coffee, sir?"

"Uh…."

"Should you prefer, there is a full selection of teas and other beverages."

If he concentrated, Royd could feel the shiftings of minute magnetic fields in the 'botler's circuits as it pondered, perhaps accessing distant databases. "We can provide warm Taarlan root beer, if that is your custom."

Royd nodded. "Yes, that would be fine."

Gael made a face. "Yuck."

Royd stuck out his tongue. "Just wait 'til you try it. You'll never drink that bitter black stuff again."

Royd's root beer arrived so quickly that he knew it had to be replicated—but it tasted so much like the real thing that he felt a twinge of homesickness.

After he'd had a few bites, he became aware of Gael peering at him over her stack of pancakes. Cocking her head, she asked, "How did you sleep last night?"

"Beautifully." He blushed. "I had some crazy dreams." And he had, indeed. His sleep had been filled with images of his trip, of the rescue at Terraport…and of Gael and Iris as well.

Gael looked down. "You too, eh?"

Together, Gael and Royd turned their eyes on Iris.

Patting her lips nonchalantly with a napkin, Iris sat back in her chair. "I did not do a thing. Whatever dreams you had, they came from your own unconscious. I am not responsible."

Gael shook her head. "I couldn't get the two of you out of my mind. It's like we…belong together."

Royd felt a tingle, and he didn't think it came from Gael's electricity.

"I'm serious," Gael continued. "We've got something special here. Don't tell me you can't feel it."

Iris narrowed her eyes. "We all had a very big day yesterday, filled with new experiences. It is no wonder that we—"

"It's more than than," Gael protested. "Yesterday, when we were in action—I've never felt so confident, so right." She looked toward Royd, as if seeking his support.

"I felt that way too," he agreed. "And more. I know it was me acting, but I also felt as if I was…I don't know, acting on behalf of something…outside me. Something larger." He chuckled nervously. "Listen to me, I sound like some kind of spiritual nut."

"No, not at all." Iris put her hand atop his, as if that were the most natural thing in the world to do. "It is the telepathic rapport you were feeling." She touched Gael with her other hand. "When we left the shuttle, we were still in a level-one rapport…just sharing surface thoughts and emotions. On the ramp, when I felt those two planning to shoot De' Artveldt—I flipped us into a level-three. It was automatic."

"What's the difference?" Royd asked.

"In level-three, all our mental abilities are shared. It is what the Institute calls `gestalt rapport.'" She held Royd's eyes, her face earnest. "You *were* feeling something larger. We all were. There was synergy going on—the whole was greater than the sum of its parts." She looked away. "I…I should not have done it. Not that deep, not with untrained and unprepared minds. I apologize."

Gael gripped Iris's hand. "Don't. We're a team. Would two untrained minds have gone so deeply into rapport if they weren't ready for it?"

"N-no. I do not think so."

"If we weren't, somehow, compatible—it couldn't have happened, could it?"

I…I do not know.

Gael smiled. **See? We're doing it now. We're a unit, a Triad. Better…more…than what we can be alone.** "I'm telling you, this was meant to be."

The 'botler interrupted them with a sound amazingly like a man clearing his throat. "Excuse me. De' Lovan has just messaged that he will arrive in one half hour, to escort you to your meeting with De' Artveldt. Perhaps you will wish to prepare?"

Gael pulled her hand back. "Good gods, yes!" She looked down at herself. "What are we going to wear?"

"Your luggage has arrived, Miss, and has been placed in your room. If you prefer, we can replicate new clothing for you. Cleaning facilities and a full stock of cosmetics are also available."

Gael wolfed down the rest of her pancakes. "Half an hour? I'll never make it."

❖

Colleen Artveldt's private office was spare yet comfortable, done in steel and rich dark wood. She met the teens at the door and waved them to a couch. "Thank you for coming. Sit down, make yourselves comfortable." To Lovan, she said, "That's all. Hold my calls and don't allow anyone to disturb us."

"Don't you want me to—"

"That's all, Stan."

Without another word, Lovan withdrew. De' Artveldt leaned against a chair, crossing her arms. "I want to thank you three once again for saving my life yesterday. But that isn't why I called you here."

She leaned forward. "I have a proposition for you. And I want you to think seriously about it."

"Okay," Gael said, speaking for them all.

De' Artveldt held up a palm terminal. "I had my staff prepare a presentation for you." She punched a button. "Watch this."

In the air before them, the stylized insignia of Artveldt Enterprises appeared, then melted into the face of a sober-looking man in a white lab coat.

"Twenty years ago, Jemalli Fever struck the Myriad Worlds. Beginning on Mars, it swept the human population and touched every known planet and colony. In the five years that the epidemic raged, three billion people died and countless others were left permanently scarred. It took the combined efforts of scientists on Earth, Aarnal, and Ixtal to develop a defense against the Jemalli Fever virus. All told, this epidemic was the worst disaster the human race has faced in over a century."

The view changed to a population graph. "Following the epidemic, the birthrate throughout the Myriad Worlds increased dramatically. The next decade and a half of accelerated birthrate, commonly referred to as the 'Baby Boom,' is the eighth such event in the last six hundred years."

A new face appeared, an exotic-looking human male with dark blue skin and white hair. A subtitle identified him as Doctor Isaac Mbouti of the Johns Hopkins Genetic Institute.

"The constellation of viruses that caused the Jemalli Fever," Doctor Mbouti said, "Had a tendency to splice a bit of its own genetic makeup into certain specific sites on the twelfth, sixteenth, and eighteenth human chromosomes. Some of these sites have been associated with psionic abilities. My work predicts that increased psionic ability occurs in approximately one in two thousand fifteen children of Jemalli Fever survivors." Doctor Mbouti looked directly at the camera, the corners of his mouth twitching in the bare outline of a grin. "The incidence in the human population, according to the latest figures, runs to about one in twenty-five thousand. I believe I have identified a major effect of the Jemalli Fever."

There followed a quick montage of news headlines and sober-faced commentators giving statistics. Juvenile crime was up 320% over the last fifteen years. Murder, suicide, and mental illness rates among teenagers had risen alarmingly in the last few years. The Galactic economy, already damaged by the Fever, was reeling under the impact of new baby boom teeners.

Orphanages were bursting at the seams, social welfare agencies were throwing up their hands, unable to cope. Planet after planet sent urgent requests for aid to the Myriad Worlds Government, to Earth, to Artveldt Enterprises, to anyone who would listen.

A year ago, in its State of the Worlds Speech, the Galactic Co-Ordinator had said, "This evening, throughout the Myriad Worlds, an entire generation is at risk. Already, we have lost far too many of our children; if we do not act, and act quickly, we may lose them all. Gentlebeings of the Assembly, time is growing short. If we do not save our children, then Posterity will, deservedly, judge us harshly. Let us join together, for the sake of these most innocent of citizens, and act now."

Three months later, that Galactic Co-Ordinator had been defeated in election. Its successor said nothing and done less about children at risk.

The holo faded and De' Artveldt stood in front of the three teens. "You three are the first wave of what's being called At Risk Generation. You're smart, self-reliant, and gifted with psi Talents that the rest of us can't imagine."

Royd shook his head. "Begging your pardon, De' Artveldt, but everyone on Taarla has some form of magnetic sensitivity."

Artveldt nodded. "Yes, of course. But not one in a thousand can manipulate magnetic fields the way you can. Your father was an ironball champion; but you scored easily twice as high as he did when you were last tested." She turned to Iris. "Iris, you were in the top five of your class at the Telepathic Institute…but did you know that even the weakest telepath in your class is stronger than the number one telepath ten years ago?"

"I did not know that."

"Gael, we don't even have to discuss your case. You and your siblings have a rare and powerful psi Talent, one that has never showed up in your family before." De' Artveldt gestured to the window and the city beyond. "There are thousands more like you—kids with weird Talents, powers that can get them into all sorts of trouble." She shrugged. "Powers that *are* getting them into trouble. They're calling you a generation at risk; I want the three of you to help me cut down those risks. And do a little good at the same time."

Gael leaned forward. "Keep talking."

"A few months ago my company got a contract from the Earth Government to work on a solution to the at-risk generation. We have a few plans." She looked from one to the other. "Have any of you ever heard of Sir Robert Baden-Powell?" The teens shook their heads. "No, I suppose not. Sir Robert was an Englishman of the Nineteenth and early Twentieth Centuries. He, too, was faced by a generation of young people at risk—he and his wife created the Boy Scouts and Girl Scouts."

Royd brightened. "Like in the old holos. Camping trips and cookie sales, Good Deed A Day and helping old people across the street, and all that rot?"

"It was a bit more complex than that, but yes, that's the idea. Scouting gave kids discipline, taught them how to deal with their abilities, and gave them something to do to keep them out of trouble." She glanced at a terminal on her desk. "I've had Research put together examples from practically every other era. The Civilian Conservation Corps, the Young Astronauts Corps, the Martian Junior Colonists, the Order of the Star—yours isn't the first generation to present the problem of at-risk children and teenagers."

"Is that what your company's working on? Bringing back the Boy Scouts and Girl Scouts?"

The woman smiled. "It's one of the ideas. Our Youth Services Division has a plan for an organization called the Youth Corps."

Gael sat back. "So what do you want us to do?"

De' Artveldt smiled. "I want you to use your Talents to do good in this world...and, not incidentally, to publicize the Youth Corps. You made a splendid start yesterday. Continue along the same lines." She sighed. "Previous ages had their Champions...psi-gifted, selfless people who put their lives on the line to help others in need. Earth's last Champion was Starfire, and she retired before you were even born. Well, it's time to bring back the age of Champions."

Royd couldn't hold back a laugh. "Starfire was the most powerful woman on the planet. And she was a 'dult. We're just kids."

"So was Starfire, when she started her career. She was only eighteen when she discovered that alien machine and gained her powers."

"I'm only fifteen," Gael protested. "Royd's younger."

Artveldt waved her objection aside. "You've heard of the Twentieth Century Champion Power Woman?"

"Who hasn't? She was the greatest Champion of them all."

"And she was 'only fifteen' when she started her career. Her cousin went public as Power Lad when he was twelve." De' Artveldt stared hard at Gael. "Don't tell me it can't be done."

There was a pause, then Iris said softly, "Tell us what you want us to do."

"Artveldt Enterprises will sponsor the Youth Corps. You three will be founding members. Eventually we'll have chapters on every world, with trained adult advisors—but kids will run the organization themselves. It's the only way to have them learn to be responsible." She looked off into the distance, seeing something that none of the teens could see. "But you three will be part of something special, a smaller group of Champions: the PsiScouts. You'll be role models, inspirations to the Corps. I want everyone in the Galaxy to hear about you. And there will be others…only those who are good enough will be allowed to become PsiScouts."

"Isn't this going to cost an awful lot?"

"It's only credits," De' Artveldt said. Royd had never heard anyone talk that way about money. "You leave that to me. I just want you three to concentrate on building the best team of kids anyone has ever seen."

Iris frowned. "I would need to clear this with the Earth Police. They hold my contract."

"Not any more, my dear. Artveldt Enterprises paid off your contract last night. You are a free spirit." Artveldt turned to Royd. "Son, you came to Earth to find a job—this is likely the best offer you'll receive."

"You mean we'll get paid?" Royd couldn't help it, it just slipped out.

De' Artveldt laughed. "Well, you won't be on the payroll as such...I want your organization to be independent of my company. But I will certainly expect all three of you to draw living expenses and a basic salary from the group's appropriation. Accounting can come up with an appropriate figure, if you'd like."

"I don't know," Gael said. "I came here to search for my brother."

"And so you shall. With the resources of Artveldt Enterprises behind you. And consider: if you work hard at making the PsiScouts and the Youth Corps a success, perhaps Dwin will be attracted and come to you of his own free will."

"I guess you're right." Gael looked first at Royd, then at Iris. "What do you two think?"

I am in favor, Iris telepathed.

Sounds excellent to me, Royd answered. **Come on, Gael, you were just telling us this morning what a great team we make.**

Gael held out her hand, palm down. "All right, De' Artveldt, you've got yourself some PsiScouts in training."

Royd put his hand atop Gael's; Iris covered them both; then De' Artveldt put her own hand on top of the stack and squeezed. "We'll stage an elaborate ceremony later for the press. For now, though, welcome aboard. We'll get started immediately. What do you need first?"

Gael looked from one to the other, then shrugged. "A place to work, I guess. Some kind of headquarters."

Artveldt beamed. "Odd that you should mention that. I have a surprise for you." She lifted her eyes and called out, "Stan?"

"Yes, Colleen?" De' Lovan answered.

"Get the car ready. We're going on a trip."

❖

Frederic Auguste Bartholdi's Statue of Liberty had perished in 2283, a casualty of the Fourth World War. Tamara Imlach's 24th Century replacement, Liberty Enlightening The Stars, combined the sleek Art Deco style of an Erte design with the robotic lines of the late 21st Century CyberMech School. The result, hailed as a triumph and condemned as a travesty, stood proud and lonely on her abandoned island, largely forgotten.

It was windy on Liberty Island, and Royd shivered beneath the blue Artveldt Enterprises jacket that Colleen had handed him from a stock in the car. Liberty's gigantic feet were perched on a white marble building in the form of a gigantic colonnaded pedestal. Colleen waved at the building, her other hand firmly clenching her hat.

"If you want it, it's yours," she shouted over the wind. "The building has more space than you'll need for years. There's an observation lounge in the Statue's crown that would make a dandy main conference room. And the torch is an excellent launch platform for your ships."

"Ships?" Royd echoed.

"Spaceships. You can hardly be a Galactic organization without a way of getting around the Galaxy, can you? I've commissioned three Mark IV starsprinters—the same model that the Solar Police use."

Iris stood back, looking up at Liberty's face far above. "It is beautiful. You mean this can be ours?"

"It *is* yours, if you want it. My Legal Department cleared everything with the government. If you want to move in, we can have a construction crew here by noon. Just say the word."

"All right," Gael said, "We'll take it."

❖

Colleen Artveldt's car flew arrow-straight toward the Manhattan dome. Stan Lovan sat up front, wearing the control glove and tensely poised as if ready to take over from the autopilot at any second.

The teens sat in the back with De' Artveldt, still trying to get used to what had happened. Royd's head was spinning— so many things to think about, so much to do. How would they ever get it all together?

"I've scheduled a press conference for noon," De' Artveldt boomed. "We'll announce the founding of the PsiScouts and talk a little about the Youth Corps. Let the media get to know you three. By nightfall the news will be on every planet in the Myriad Worlds. You'll have your first applicants for membership tomorrow morning, unless I miss my guess."

"What are we going to do with them?" Gael asked.

"That's entirely up to you," De' Artveldt answered.

That is hardly helpful, Iris thought.

Royd, though, was ready for the question. The organization of the new group was one of the things he'd been pondering. "I think we're going to need a lot of help. What about two levels of membership? We should pick and train the kids who will actually run the Youth Corps—call them Cadets—ourselves, and as soon as we can."

Gael frowned. "We're going to be awfully busy, if we anticipate chapters on each planet."

"No," Iris said, "We start small. Once the Cadets are trained, we'll send them out to start offworld chapters. Soon the process will run itself. Go on, Royd, what's your third level?"

"Uh…I don't have a name for them yet. They'd be the ones we're really after, the at-risk kids who need to learn self-discipline and how to stay out of trouble."

"Champions," Gael suggested.

Royd gestured, indicating the three levels. "When things get under way, kids will join as Champions. Those who show the most ability will move up to be Cadets. And anyone with psi Talents is a candidate to become a PsiScout." He stopped, gnawing his lip. "Hmmm. I guess eventually we'll have a corps of PsiScouts on each planet…if we have enough who can make it."

De' Artveldt smiled. "I don't think that will be a problem for quite a while. I think you'll find that you three are rarer than you think." She reached for a terminal. "Marketing has designed some new outfits for you to wear. I thought you'd want to—"

"Hold on!"

Lovan's shout caught them all by surprise. Royd grabbed a handhold and reached out to steady De' Artveldt.

"There…ahead!"

Only twenty meters away, a huge cargo truck had bolted from oncoming traffic and was bearing straight toward them, hell-bent on collision.

Lovan moved quickly, and at the last possible second the car dropped a dozen meters. Royd screamed, and the truck raced past overhead with only centimeters of clearance.

Caught in the truck's backwash, the car tumbled while Lovan fought for control. They plummeted, then pulled up sharply, so close to the water that Royd was sure he saw a fish.

He felt Iris's mental influence calming him.

"Damn!" Lovan said. "That idiot could have killed us. Where did he go?"

Very quietly, Iris answered, "I see him." During the whole confusing tumble, she had kept her eyes firmly on the careening truck.

"Aren't we going to follow him?" Royd said.

"Not with De' Artveldt aboard," Lovan snapped. "I'm getting her to safety right away." With that, he turned the car and accelerated toward the city.

"But the truck's going to get away," Gael protested.

"No, he is not," Iris said firmly. In another moment, an Earth Police car appeared, as if from nowhere, and raced after the truck.

"Now where were they when we needed them?" Lovan grumbled.

"I made mental contact with the Police and relayed the sight of the truck. That officer was off-duty but in the neighborhood."

By this time they reached the dome and entered through an arched gate. In a moment, two Artveldt Enterprises cars paced them, and stayed until they reached De' Artveldt's building.

Lovan fumed in quiet as they rode up in the elevator, but once they reached Artveldt's office he exploded. "Dammit, Colleen, now you *have* to listen to me. That truck driver was out to kill you. That makes two attempts on your life in two days." Belatedly, he noticed Royd and the others. "Look, could you please make these kids leave?"

Artveldt stood her ground, arms crossed. "No, I will not." Her face softened. "Stan, I appreciate your concern, but we have a lot of work to do. The press conference is in less than two hours."

"You're not still going to hold that conference?! After what just happened?"

Gael hesitantly said, "De' Artveldt, if you'd rather, we can postpone the conference…."

Artveldt closed her eyes and took a deep breath. After a few seconds, she exhaled. "Thank you, Gael, but that won't be necessary. Stan is very concerned, but really, there's no reason to worry."

"No reason to worry?" Lovan shook his head. "I don't believe you, Colleen. Obviously someone wants you dead—to show up at a preannounced press conference would be to walk into a trap."

"I don't believe that I'm in danger here, in my own corporate headquarters." She sighed. "We can't even be sure that this latest incident was deliberate. Before we panic, let's see what the Police have to say." Her face grew hard again. "Now the Scouts and I have a lot of work to do; we'd appreciate privacy. Please see that we're not disturbed."

"Colleen...." He closed his mouth, then spun on a heel and marched out. The door clicked shut behind him.

"De' Artveldt," Royd said, "Maybe you should be more careful...."

Artveldt grimaced. "Now, Royd, don't *you* start in on me too. I've lived through worse periods than this. I'll survive." She strode to her desk and tapped a code into her terminal. "Wait until you see the clothes our Marketing Division has designed for you."

Holos appeared, full-size virtual duplicates of Royd, Gael, and Iris in their new finery. The images rotated slowly to show all sides.

Each outfit was different in style and colors, yet they were all obviously related. Their lines—loose-fitting, with large pockets, epaulets, substantial boots—recalled military uniforms...but the costumes were brightly-colored and obviously very comfortable. Royd's was a deep maroon accented in a light grey.

"Nice," Gael said. Her intended outfit was two-toned, light and dark shades of a deep, almost turquoise green. The holo's hair, the same bright red as Gael's, blazed against the costume.

Iris stood back, a dubious expression on her face and her arms folded as she surveyed her own jet-black uniform. "Why the red and white stripes?"

Narrow piping in scarlet and white trimmed the arms, shoulders, and legs of each uniform.

"That's one of the elements that tie them all together," Artveldt answered. "We wanted to indicate that you're all on the same team. The patches serve the same function."

Royd looked closer. Chest patches, identical on all three outfits, bore a stylized outline of the Statue of Liberty. Above the right breast was another patch: Royd's bore a symbolic horseshoe magnet, Gael's featured a stylized lightning bolt, and Iris's was the Greek psi. Above these ID patches were name tags.

"Marketing also thought you should have new names to match your public personae." Artveldt sighed. "I can tell you, you'll appreciate them a lot more in the future. You can't know how tired you get of playing the celebrity game, of having no privacy. Public aliases will make it a little easier for you."

Now Gael frowned. "All right, what names did Marketing come up with?"

"Gael, they want to call you 'Bolt.' Iris, you'll be known as 'Mentaxa.' And Royd, your new name is 'Coulomb.'"

"Bolt, eh?" Gael's frown faded. "I guess it could be worse."

Royd was less happy. "What's a Coulomb?"

"It's the unit of measure for electric charge. Electricity in motion—"

Royd nodded. "Creates magnetism." He frowned. "Why not 'Tesla'? That's the unit of magnetic flux."

"It's also a particularly naughty word in the language of Tromblor."

"Oh. Coulomb, eh? All right, I guess I'll give it a try."

"Good, I was afraid you wouldn't like them."

Iris was still frowning at her outfit. "Personally, I think the stripes are dorky." She squinted. "But otherwise, they look fairly good. Who designed them?"

"We contracted Banarp ube'Nalic for the original designs. She did the concept sketches herself, then assigned one of her best designers to us for the rest."

Gael whistled. "You go right to the top, don't you?"

"Nothing's too good for the PsiScouts. We want the public to notice you and remember you; nothing gets noticed and remembered better than a ube'Nalic design." Artveldt touched another code on her terminal. "All sorts of accessories are available. Jackets, vests, headgear, scarves, gloves—you'll have a full choice. And if you want anything that's not included, just ask."

A robot clothes rack rolled in, crammed with the new uniforms and accessories. "Why don't you try them on?" Artveldt offered. "There's a bathroom through here, and you can also use the conference room next door."

When the three had changed, Royd was amazed at how good the costumes looked on them. Whoever made them had known the teens' measurements to the centimeter. Royd held up his arms and pirouetted before a holomirror. "I'm lookin' good," he said.

"You'll do," Gael answered. Her hair, set off by a turquoise headband, was liquid fire against the costume.

Iris stretched, then bent and touched her toes. Straightening up, she announced, "There is more to these outfits than meets the eye."

"You're right." Artveldt reached into a pocket and produced a laser knife, which she dialed to minimum dispersion. "Watch."

She turned the knife on Royd's forearm. Instantly the whole arm of his suit turned mirror-silver, reflecting the beam away.

"Intelligent fabric," Artveldt said. "Adjusts its own reflectivity to protect against energy weapons or shield you from radar and ladar. You've also noticed that it adjusts its fit automatically."

"Nice," Gael said.

"Here." De' Artveldt handed Iris a length of metal pipe. "Try to hit Royd with this."

Iris swung, but the pipe stopped a half-dozen centimeters from Royd's stomach, then slowly swung to touch him.

"Class One inertial damper field; you're protected from minor impacts and small projectile weapons." Artveldt reached out a hand, slowly, and touched Royd's shoulder. "Slow-moving objects aren't affected by the field."

Gael looked in wonder at her costume. "What other surprises are there?"

"The fabric is temperature-sensitive and will adjust itself to keep you comfortable. You can go into space with them, or dive down to three hundred meters in the ocean. Gloves and transparent hood will form automatically when they're needed. You're also wired for secure, scrambled communication between yourselves, and you have Net access via an onboard computer system. The batteries last fifty hours, and they are on constant automatic recharge whenever you're within range of a power source."

Royd looked up from his suit. "Can it make me fly?" he asked, with a twinkle in his eye.

"We're still working on that," De' Artveldt answered.

Iris pulled on a cape, floor-length and black as coal. It swirled around her ankles as she walked from one end of the room to the other. Then, grudgingly, she smiled. "All right, I suppose this will do."

"Glad to hear it." Artveldt took the laser knife back from Royd. "Now that you're garbed, maybe you have a better idea of why I think Stan is overreacting to this assassination nonsense?"

Gael saw it first. "Your clothes give the same protection. You weren't in danger in the car...or at the spaceport yesterday."

Royd looked at Artveldt's clothing, a conservative business suit in dark wine red, with new eyes.

"Correction," De' Artveldt said. "If the car had exploded, or if that truck had crushed us, my suit would be no protection. And I wasn't wearing a protective suit when I got off the shuttle—so they'd have had me then." She shook her head. "Royd...I mean, Coulomb...what time is it?"

"Huh? I don't—" Suddenly, he did know, as a computer voice whispered in his ear. "Ten minutes to noon."

"All right, children, it's time. Are you ready for this press conference?"

They exchanged glances, then Gael said, "As ready as we'll ever be."

"Fine. Let's go downstairs, then, and get it over with."

❖

The press was less than kind. In fact, many of the reporters treated the whole conference as a joke, and some of them were unmerciful.

"De' Artveldt," one asked, "Will you be encouraging your PsiScouts to do one good deed a day, or will the quota be higher?"

Artveldt laughed. "We're hoping they'll be too busy to worry about things like that."

"Miss…uh…Mentaxa? Suppose one of our viewers needs to call on your services. Let's say there's a cat up a tree, or an old person who help across the street? How should they get in touch with you?"

Royd felt Iris inwardly shrink back from the attack, although physically she didn't move. "Our netcode appears in the directories," she answered.

A short, balding man stood up and cleared his throat. "I'm Fein Thegkif of MWNN. De' Artveldt, don't you think it's a little irresponsible of you to encourage these children in playing at their little super-hero club? After all, it's a dangerous Galaxy out there. What happens when your kids get themselves into some kind of trouble that they can't handle? Who's going to be stuck with bailing them out?"

Artveldt nodded toward the teens. "De' Thegkif, I think we should let them answer that."

Thanks a lot! Gael surged forward, eyes flashing; Royd restrained her with a hand on her shoulder and stepped forward instead.

"Ahem," he said, "De' Thegkif, that's a very good question. I'm sure it's on a lot of minds. You said 'irresponsible' and you called us 'children'…for far too long, my generation has been branded with those words. Irresponsible. Uncontrollable. Wild, disrespectful, impatient, ungracious, rude, uncivilized. And we've lived up to those words. We've taken them all on ourselves and acted proud of it. Maybe it's because we were never taught any different."

Royd straightened his back and looked directly into Thegkif's video pickup, uncomfortably aware that he was addressing millions of viewers throughout the Myriad Worlds. "Well, here stand three kids who aren't going to accept those words anymore. We're going to be take responsibility for ourselves, and we're going to show other kids how to do the same. That's what the Youth Corps and the PsiScouts are all about. If you think we're just children playing super-hero...well, then, it's up to us to prove you wrong. All we ask is the chance to prove ourselves."

When Royd sat down, there was a hush in the room.

De' Artveldt stepped into the void, smiling. "If there are no further questions...?" There were none. "Thank you all for your attention. Requests for private interviews should be made through my press liaison, De' Jenthen. Once again, thank you."

Gently but firmly, Artveldt steered the teens through a connecting door and into a service corridor. A young, darkskinned man, barely out of his teens, slouched against the wall. He wore loose, casual khakis and sturdy boots. From his left ear, the gold-plated hardware of a full Net link dangled like a trophy on display to the world.

"Hiya, Colleen," he said, falling into step beside her. "Tough audience back there."

"They'll come around."

Still walking, the young man turned around and offered his hand to the teens. "Pleased to meet you, PsiScouts. I'm Jav Emry. I'm netjay for alt.trends.commentary on EarthNet. I want to apologize for the behavior of my colleagues back there. Most of 'em haven't joined the human race yet." Before any of them could answer, Jav continued, "Hey, any chance of me scheduling an interview or RTC with you three? I know my group would love to talk to you."

De' Artveldt smiled as she interrupted Jav's rapid-fire delivery. "You wouldn't know it to look at him, but Jav's one of the real opinion-makers here on Terra. I'd take him up on his offer, if I were you."

Jav bowed his head. "Colleen, you say the sweetest things." He looked at Gael. "So, what about it?"

Gael shrugged. "Sure. When?"

Jav closed his eyes for a moment, then reopened them and said, "Need some lead time to talk it up, get people interested. Hmm, I'll run a bulletin twice an hour, drop mail to my regulars, run a drone down to get some shots of the new HQ of yours—say, eight tonight?"

"That's kinda soon," Royd said.

They reached an elevator; Jav followed them in, relaxed against the acceleration surge. "If you want, we can put it off for an hour or three. I'd hate to delay any longer; those other guys are going to be using the PsiScouts for silly-season fodder all afternoon." He frowned. "I wish I could put y'all on sooner, actually, but my sims say that until eight, you're not news. And by eleven, unless we go on, you're the day's hot joke."

The elevator opened on the reception area of De' Artveldt's office. A small crowd was waiting for Artveldt; she turned to Stan Lovan, pointedly leaving the teens alone with Jav.

She is making it obvious that this is our decision, Iris thoughtcast.

Jav knows what he's talking about, Gael answered. **If you two are nervous, we can do the interview in rapport....**

Jav looked from Gael to Iris. "Hey, Mentaxa, you're doing the telepath thing right now, aren't you? This is great! I clipped video; can I use it in my promos? Wait, I know, we can get shots of each of you using your Talents. Spot the clips on other SIGs, one-second subliminals, I have a dæmon to do that for me. All I need to do is schedule a definite time, and we're set."

Gael nodded. "Eight tonight is fine for us."

"Good. I'll blink your netcodes to remind you about half an hour before. For video, we can either use a phone pickup, or I can send a drone, or we can meet at your HQ. Whatever's more convenient for you." He rubbed his hands together. "This is going to be great. My suscribers'll love it."

"Jav," Royd said, "Do you mind if I ask you a question?"

"You just did, Coulomb m'boy. Go ahead, hit me with another."

It was impossible not to smile. "Okay. All the other reporters were…I don't know…almost laughing at us."

"And you want to know why I'm not?"

"Uh-huh."

"Fair question." Jav looked very earnest. "I started out as a netjay when I was fifteen. I can still remember how much grief I took from the 'dults—they just weren't willing to believe that a kid could handle things responsibly. So I guess I'm batting for you three because I wish someone had been in there batting for me." He shrugged. "Besides, the PsiScouts are news. And that's my business. Think of it, my SIG will have the first exclusive interview with the founding members. When you take off, like I'm sure you will, that will bring us plenty of new subscribers." Jav peered past Royd at the crowd surrounding Artveldt. "Hell. That's Chief of Police Ormandeau. What's he doing here?"

At the same moment, De' Artveldt beckoned to the teens. "Come over, you'll want to hear this." Jav tagged along.

The Police Chief was short, fat, and vaguely oriental. A grey Police dress uniform hugged his bulging shoulders and abdomen. His left eye was partially obscured by a data monocle.

"Chief Ormandeau," De' Artveldt said, "Meet Bolt, Coulomb, and Mentaxa. Go ahead, continue with what you were saying."

The Chief cleared his throat. "My department has investigated that truck that almost ran you down, and I thought I would come in person to tell you what we've found out." He shot a stern look at Jav. "This isn't for publication, lad."

Jav spread his hands. "You're thinking of someone else, Chief. I never make privates public."

"Well, you'd better not in this case, or I will prosecute."

"Chief," De' Artveldt prompted, "If you don't mind…?"

"Did you find the truck driver?" Gael asked.

"That's the thing," the Chief said. "There *was* no driver. The truck was remotely-controlled."

"Could you track the origin of the controlling signal?" Iris asked.

The Chief shook his head. "By the time we got to it, the trail was cold. I'm sorry, De'—you know I hate to give negative results."

Artveldt sighed heavily. "And I suppose there's been no more news from the two the PsiScouts apprehended at the spaceport, eh?"

"None at all. It looks as if they were hypno-conditioned to give us false leads." His brow wrinkled. "If we only had some sense of motive, or some feeling for what the perpetrators want…."

"Isn't that obvious, Chief? They want me dead."

"That's the most logical assumption. But I wish I knew for sure. Can you think of anything that someone might be trying to scare you off of, anything somebody doesn't want you doing?"

Artveldt laughed. "Half of what the company does is unpopular with one weirdo or another. I don't have anything in particular, no."

"Then I'll repeat my offer of a couple officers as bodyguards." The Chief half-frowned at the teens, and Royd didn't need Mentaxa's telepathy to see that he didn't think too highly of teenagers, even if they did have special Talents.

Iris, wouldn't you have just loved working for him? You're lucky we rescued you, Gael thought.

I have no comment about that.

De' Artveldt gave the smile that Royd was already beginning to recognize as her enough-is-enough look. "I thank you for the offer. I know that your officers have many other things to do, things more important than standing guard over an old lady. I can afford my own protection—and I assure you, I've engaged the very best." She softened. "Varj, you and your troops are doing the best job you can. I don't expect the impossible."

"I *do*."

"Yes, I know. So quit it." She pressed his hand, then said, "I have two dozen other people waiting for me. Thanks for coming by in person—"

"Well, I wanted to see your little show."

"Stay and talk to the youngsters. *They're* the ones who are going to accomplish the impossible, my friend. You ought to get to know them." De' Artveldt nodded in dismissal and turned to her next supplicant.

The Chief looked distinctly uncomfortable. By unspoken agreement, the three teens smiled sweetly and said nothing, their eyes faintly expectant, letting him stew for long moments. It was Jav who finally broke the silence.

"So, Chief, off the record—what's happening that I should know about?"

"You shouldn't know about anything, Emry. You'll just blab it all on your scandal-net, and then I'll have to go to the trouble of suing you."

Jav grinned. "Tut-tut, Chief. Freedom of the Nets, remember. Come on, have a heart. It's been a slow news day. I'm putting these nice people on at eight, and if I don't have an ongoing, dramatic story running for the next few hours, I won't get any subscriber interest. So what tips can you give me?"

I'm glad Jav is on our side, Royd thought. He was learning how to pitch his thoughts so that Iris could pick them up and echo them in rapport.

Yeah, Gael answered, *Think of the damage he could do if he was against us.*

"I can't give you a thing."

"Can you let me play Twenty Questions? For instance, what's going down over in Tribeca? I've got reports of a dozen police cars landing in the last ten minutes. Something I should know?"

The Chief closed his right eye, squinting at his data monocle. After a few grunts and harumphs, he said, "You didn't hear this from me, you understand?"

"Absolutely."

"Gang war. Omicron Force has taken over the Paradise Towers complex. They're hunting down Blizzards and Powerslaves in the corridors. We're trying to establish a security cordon to keep bystanders out...then we'll move in."

"Chief, I have a report that your Hostage Response Team has landed. Is this a hostage situation?"

"Hell, you'll find out soon enough anyway. Yes. There are hostages."

"How many? Who are they?"

The Chief shook his head. "No comment." Another glance at the data monocle, then he nodded to Jav and the teens. "If you'll excuse me, I need to get to my car." Without waiting for a response, he was gone.

Jav grabbed Gael's arm. "All right, kids, let's go. Looks like you're on."

"Go?" Iris echoed. "Go where?"

"Paradise Towers. I have a story to cover, and you've got some hostages to rescue."

❖

EARTHNET alt.trends.commentary ON Tue Apr 19, 2574
Sec: 1 Conf: 1
{RTC RECEIVE ONLY}
[RUNNING ARCHIVE TO Sec: 1 Thread: 205]
** RESPOND ON Sec: 1 Conf: 6 **
FROM: NETJAY [Jav Man] AT 19:08:58
— — — — — — — — — —

   [THIS IS A REALTIME REPORT]

   This monstrosity behind me is the main entrance to the so-called Paradise Towers, where Mayor Hua's mother is a hostage of the gang known as Omicron Force. [REF: Key 814 for background OMICRON FORCE]

   The sparkle you're seeing is neither a transmission artifact nor gremlins in your eyeballs; it's a proximity defense screen enclosing the whole building. And that body draped so artfully across the entrance, is what's left of the Police officer who tried to cross the screen.

   Listen, boys and girls, this is serious business and people have gotten hurt. So use your brains — or borrow some — and stay away from Paradise Towers. Stay out of Tribeca. In fact, stay out of New York altogether. Our friends in blue-and-grey are doing the best they can; they don't need joyhoppers buzzing by to take a look. Pay attention, bobbo. This means you.

   Back to our story. The EP's have isolated Paradise Towers from all city services and Net connect. EP hostage negotiators are on a single comm line into the building, and no, you can't listen in so don't even try it. [REF: Key 166 for background PARADISE TOWERS]

   All of the residents of the lovely Towers are at risk in this crisis. Far be it for me to suggest that any citizen's life is more important than another's, but one reason you're seeing such quick and massive reaction from the EP's is the star hostage, Delia Hua. Yes, that Delia Hua: the mother of Hizzoner Clement Hua, by the grace of several gods the current Mayor of New York and Chair of the Earth Council. [REF: Key 706 for background DELIA HUA] [REF: Key 233 for background MAYOR CLEMENT HUA]

As EP negotiators attempt to earn their salaries and the world holds its breath—all except for two dingbrains in Bogota who still don't get it—three daring teenagers have entered Paradise Towers in an attempt to shut down the defense screen and rescue the Mayor's Mama. I can tell you this only because the gangers are cut off and can't get a word I say.

You may not have heard of the PsiScouts before, my droogs and drooglets, but I'm betting they'll be on every tongue on the planet by tomorrow. And remember, you saw it here first. [REF: Key 001 for background PSISCOUTS]

Stay linked, chilluns, for further developments.

— — — — — — — — — —

❖

Getting through the proximity screen was easy. Royd crouched with the others behind Paradise Towers, out of sight behind a garbage bin, and felt for the magnetic shape of the field. Then he nodded. *Okay, I can match it long enough to get us in. What then?*

Gael glanced forward and back. *Iris?*

Mentaxa. This is official business, after all. Mentally, Iris conveyed a smile that belied the deadpan expression on her face.

I don't care who you are, I just want to know if you're ready.

Nada problem. I did this all the time at school, whenever a few of us wanted to sneak out. Once Coulomb gets us through that screen, we could dance naked on the loading dock and nobody would notice us.

All right. Double-time across the grass and through that archway. Royd—sorry, Coulomb—you unlock the door, and as soon as we're inside, Mentaxa can drop her mind-shield. Good? Good. Let's go!

It worked perfectly. The lock was simple, hardly worth the effort it took to spring it. Royd briefly considered the possibility that there would be an alarm, then realized that no one would be watching for it—why bother, when they had the proximity screen?

The door opened into a large, dark delivery area; Gael immediately waved Royd and Iris to a secluded position behind a stack of boxes.

We need to find De' Hua and the other hostages first, Gael thought. *Any ideas?*

Iris frowned. *Too many minds for me to pick out specific thoughts. I would need to be within ten meters or so.*

Right. Before entering, Gael had downloaded the building's plans; she displayed a 3D model against the stained concrete floor. *Those express elevators: one at each corner. If we rode up one and down the other, do you think you'd be able to pick out the floor they're on?*

Iris shook her head. *Probably. But I do not like it. Too many people running around; there are three gangs fighting over this turf. We could not guarantee that we would have an elevator to ourselves.*

Royd squinted at the display. *What about the robot accessways? They open on every floor, and there sure aren't going to be humans to see us in there.*

How will you keep the robots from throwing us out?, Iris asked.

Royd just grinned. *Robots and I go back a long way.*

❖

Silently, swiftly, the PsiScouts prowled the hidden access tunnels of Paradise Towers. They kept low, sometimes creeping on hands and knees or squeezing through openings hardly larger than their shoulders. The accessways were dark, but Royd found that his suit contained infrared goggles.

Pausing now and again to consult the plans, they moved in great counterclockwise squares around each floor, then clung to vertical conveyors to move up to the next level. When they met a maintenance robot, Royd or Gael quickly dispatched it with a magnetic pulse or electrical blast.

By the time they reached the top of the building, Iris had an accurate census of residents and interlopers from each of the three gangs. Omicron Force controlled floors twenty to fifty; Blizzard and Powerslaves had formed an uneasy alliance to defend eight through twelve. The other floors were no-man's-land where fearful residents crouched behind their locked doors and listened anxiously to Omicron Force blustering on the building's internal nets.

De' Artveldt is right, Iris thought. *It sickens me that these gangers are all our age or younger. There are kids seven and eight years old in here—shooting at one another!*

Give us some time, girl! Have you found the hostages?

That way, I believe.

Bolt eased an access panel open just a crack, and they all crowded around to peer through.

"'Dults," Bolt whispered. "They're 'dults."

Hush.

Half a dozen 'dults sat against one wall of a large room; through Mentaxa's power, Royd could feel their fear and helplessness. Three hooded women stood stiffly, weapons held on the six hostages.

Look at the woman in the middle. Isn't she Delia Hua?

Royd consulted the digitized image that Jav had given them. *Yup, that's her.*

Besides the guards, there were two other 'dults in the room. Gael immediately tagged them Pigman and Stinky. Both were hunched over a terminal, talking.

His suit's comm unit had built-in sound pickups; Royd tuned them higher and strained to make out the pair's words over amplified background noise.

"...Half a million credits and transport to Triton," Stinky was saying.

They're talking to the Police negotiators.

Royd couldn't make out the Police response, but apparently Stinky wasn't satisfied. "No Earth interference on Triton. All Police forces have to withdraw within the next 24 hours."

"You have fifteen minutes," Pigman said. "Then we'll start killing our guests. One at a time, every fifteen minutes."

The Police said something else, then Stinky snarled, "Then get the Mayor on this channel, and quit wasting my time." She punched the terminal, and the screen went blank.

Bolt eased the access panel shut. *Withdraw, kids. We need to plan strategy.*

We do not have time, Mentaxa thought. *They will start killing people in fifteen minutes.*

Then we've got ten minutes. Let's use it.

She's right, Royd agreed. *Follow me.*

Ten meters down, the accessway opened into a larger volume, a maintenance junction crowded with readouts and control panels. Careful to touch nothing, Royd settled his back against the wall and sat down hard.

"So what are we going to do?" Bolt asked, crouching.

Mentaxa frowned. "What do you suggest?"

"Can you knock them out with some kind of telepathic thingie?"

"No. Too many. Two, three maybe...but not five." She looked up, as if listening, then turned suddenly to Coulomb. "What do you think?"

"I don't know. I—" *Royd, keep talking. Say anything, but make it sound as if you are planning.* "—I guess one option is to just burst in and try to knock out as many of them as we can. Bolt can shock them, you can do your telepathic business, I could try to get their weapons away from them...."

As he spoke, he was aware of Iris's voice echoing in his mind. *I sense someone else in this chamber with us. Someone invisible. I am trying to get an idea of their position. Bolt, be ready.*

"...But that way, we're still taking the risk that they're going to start shooting people."

Right behind you, Gael. One...two...NOW!

Lightning played from Gael's hands and shoulders, strobe-lighting the narrow chamber and leaving the afterimage impression of a short person, hands reaching toward Gael's neck.

As soon as they started, the pyrotechnics were over. Gael leaped up and spun, grabbing a suddenly-visible girl ganger. She seemed barely as old as Royd himself.

"Talk," Gael hissed, sparks crackling in her hair. "Who are you and what are you doing here?"

"Omicron Force rules!" the girl answered defiantly. "My mates will be after me second or two."

"I doubt it," Gael answered. "I asked you a question."

"I'm Tovi, of Omicron Force, and ye ain't gettin' nothin' else out of me."

She is very confident. She keeps thinking just a few more minutes, and she will get away. She... Iris's face wrinkled in concentration. **...She has the ability to turn invisible and intangible. Like a ghost. Hold her. Royd, give me some light.**

Royd punched a control on his belt, and the white stripes of his uniform glowed, shedding enough light to read by.

Iris grabbed Tovi's chin in her hand and stared into the girl's eyes. After a moment or two, she dropped her hand. "You can let her go, Bolt. She is not going anywhere now."

The girl's eyes, unblinking, stayed locked on Iris's. "What are ye, a witch?" She squirmed, but was unable to break Iris's control.

"A telepath," Mentaxa answered. "Bolt, we do not have time to fool with this baggage. I am going to put her to sleep."

"Wait," Royd said. "I think she might be able to help us."

"Ain't helpin' no fuggin' Blizzard trash."

"We aren't Blizzards and we're not Powerslaves either. We're...the new gang on the scene. PsiScouts." He eyed the girl, trying to look tough. "You're kinda young for an Omicron."

"Am not. I'm Force Strike Leader this operation."

"Are you, now? What's Omicron Force trying to accomplish here?"

The girl shook, struggling not to answer, but Mentaxa's mental influence was obviously too strong. "Zards grabbed Paradise Towers last year. This is Omicron Force turf. We just tryin' to get back what's ours."

"Then who are those 'dults with hostages next door?"

"Few weapons dealers we brought along. Co-ordinate hardware, set up prox-screen, calm down residents. Listen," she pleaded, "We don't want nobody hurt save Zards and Slaves. Figure rezzies'll listen to 'dults. Don't know nothin' about hostages."

Gael gave a tight-lipped smile. "Girl, you and your precious Omicron Force have been had. Those weapons dealers are in the other room negotiating for half a million credits and transport to Triton." She laughed, cold and dry. "They used you to get in here and take their hostages. And they're going to leave you holding the bag when the cops move in."

"Ain't true."

"If you'll shut up," Royd said, "We'll show you."

❖

Five minutes later, the four stood around a table in a conference room that adjoined the hostage chamber. Three other kids, Tovi's lieutenants, listened intently as she barked orders, backing them up with sharp, quick gestures.

"Find generators, cut 'em. No power this floor. Gather up guns, bring 'em here. Halt all fightin', Zards and Slaves send someone in charge up here—safe passage. Kick any Cron 'at gives trouble. Scat!"

"Cutting power won't save the hostages," Gael said.

"Will keep dealers from runnin', though. We gotta take care of hostages." She shook her head, tight curls quivering. "Mayor's mother! 'Course cops gonna be pissed. Stupid 'dults."

Five minutes left, Mentaxa anxiously thoughtcast.

"What kind of guns are they carrying?" Bolt demanded.

"Nasty. Megawatt particle packets. One hit, dead."

"Coulomb?"

"Give me a bit, boss," Royd answered. His suit's onboard computer retrieved information about particle packet guns from its encyclopedia, then displayed it before Royd's eyes. "The packets are stabilized by a transient magnetic bubble. I can probably deflect them—but I've never tried it, and I'd hate to learn by making mistakes."

Four minutes.

One of Tovi's lieutenants, a dirty-faced boy of thirteen or so, burst in. Without waiting to hear what he had to say, she spun on him and held out her hand. "Gun. Now."

The weapon he produced was plainly twin to those carried by the adult guards. Tovi grinned, then raised the gun and pointed at an empty corner of the room. "Target practice, eh?"

"No!" Gael barked. "They'll hear. Go down the hall and practice. And be quick about it."

Tovi handed Royd the gun, and he sprinted down the corridor. Various members of Omicron Force were gathering on the floor; they ignored him. Ducking into an emergency stairwell, he pointed the gun down the stairs and fired.

It took three shots before he was able to feel the shape of the magnetic field that stitched the energy packets together; five more before he learned to deflect those packets. Then, examining the gun more closely, he grinned.

Two minutes. Get back to the maintenance junction. Bolt says you had better be able to control those packets, because you are all we have.

Even better, he answered, on the run. *I found out how to set the safeties magnetically. I can do it from five meters away.*

Good. There is no time to brief you; I am taking the three of us into gestalt rapport at once.

Royd moved with a sudden consciousness of Gael and Iris crouched with Tovi behind the access panel. Through Iris's eyes, he saw Stinky and Pigman once again before the terminal, felt their anger.

On the terminal's screen, Chief Ormandeau looked pained. "You must give us more time. We've only just located the Mayor; it will take him only a few more minutes to get to a secure location to discuss your terms."

Royd ducked into the accessway and crawled forward until he was behind Tovi. Closing his eyes, he focussed on Mentaxa's view of the room. *Look at the guard on the left. I want to see her gun.* Mentaxa obeyed.

"I don't care if he's not at a secure location," Stinky snarled. "If you don't put him on right now, one of our guests will depart."

Royd concentrated, cast out his magnetic force, and felt the first safety snap closed. *Next one,* he directed Mentaxa.

"Ten seconds, Chief. Nine."

Snap. *Number three, Iris. Hurry.*

"Eight. Seven."

"I'm telling you, I can't get the Mayor on that quickly."

"Five seconds."

Damn. The third safety wouldn't move. Peering closer, Royd saw that the guard had her thumb unconsciously resting on the switch. If he threw it against her resistance, she would notice.

The gestalt—Gael, Iris, Royd—made an instant decision. *Go!*

Royd pulled, hard as he could, and the gun jerked aside. The guard fired by reflex, but the energy packet went wild and impacted on the ceiling.

At the same moment, Bolt kicked the access panel aside and jumped into the room, lightning flashing from her hands. Two guards slumped and fell, unconscious, and Royd felt the rapport tremble as waves of exhaustion swept through Mentaxa.

Tovi, half-transparent, passed through the wall and into the room. The third guard fired at her, and the energy packet flew right through her, blasting a window into shards of glass.

At that instant, the lights went out. Royd's goggles at once switched to infrared mode; he picked out the third guard and tackled her, feeling his suit stiffen around him as he and the guard hit the ground in a heap.

Lightning-strobe showed the expression of surprise on Pigman's face, the half-aimed gun in his hand, as he fell beneath Bolt's charge.

Struggling, Royd tore the guard's gun from her grip and sent it sailing out the window. Then he felt Mentaxa's presence strong behind him, and the guard went limp.

Sorry. I was not ready for the effort.

No problem. I was actually enjoying it. Gasping, Royd pulled himself up. Where was Stinky? And where was Tovi?

The access panel was swinging. Bolt gestured at it and said, "They went that way. All according to plan." Her uniform's stripes lit, a reassuring pale white, and she faced the hostages. "Don't worry, you're safe. It's over." Crossing to the door, she opened it and called out, "All right, turn the power back on."

After a few moments, the lights came up—and so did the terminal. Chief Ormandeau, red-faced, appeared in mid-scream: "—The hell is going on there?!"

Bolt forced a smile. "Not to worry, Chief. Everything is under control. Tell Mayor Hua that his mother is okay—and so are the other hostages. As soon as we can find the controls, we'll drop the proximity screen."

"B-but," Royd said, "Stinky got away."

"We hope so," Iris answered. Through the rapport, Royd saw what she meant.

He couldn't help smiling.

❖

Jav faced the drone pickup squarely and finished his report. "That concludes our coverage of the Paradise Towers gang war. I'm going to restore Real-Time Conference on this section and let you people talk for a while—then at eight we go live with the PsiScouts. Stay linked, friends and neighbors, you don't want to miss this one." He gave a great sigh and pocketed the drone, then clapped Gael on the back.

"Good job, you three." He gave Royd and Iris rough hugs. "Half the world is gonna be tuned in tonight." His smile melted away. "Too bad the one you called Stinky got away."

The teens exchanged glances. "Uh...Jav," Gael said, "Can you keep something off the air for us? Just until the situation clears up?"

"Only if you promise me exclusive coverage when it does."

"Fair enough." She lowered her voice. "We *let* Stinky get away. In fact, that's what took us so long clearing the proximity screen—we wanted to give her time to get plenty far away."

"You kids aren't turning ganger on me, are you? You don't want to mess with the Triton Liberation Front; those people are seriously brainbroke."

"No, we're not going ganger. Look—do you think Stinky and Pigman were acting on their own? Not likely. They were following somebody's orders. But whose?"

Jav shook his head. "If you knew that, Chief Ormandeau would be giving you medals instead of filing citations. The EPs have been after higher-ups in the TLF for years." He suddenly stopped. "You put a bug on Stinky. You're going to follow her to her boss. Won't work, chilluns. She'll use bugspray before she goes anywhere near De' Big. Good try, though."

Gael looked disgustingly superior. "Good. That's what we figured. That's why we planted a tracker as a decoy. She'll find it and then think it's safe to go to De' Big."

"Confess to Papa, kids. How are you tracking her if you're not using a bug?"

Briefly, Gael explained about Tovi and her ability to become invisible and intangible. "See, Stinky is much bigger than Tovi. So Tovi's…er…hiding inside Stinky. When Stinky meets up with De' Big, Tovi will leave her and give us a call."

Jav laughed. "You guys are too much. Damn, I've got to be at Police Headquarters when this breaks. I want to clip the Chief's expression and keep it on file."

❖

Jav's conference went surprisingly well. Royd fidgeted, and Iris was plainly uncomfortable under all the attention… but Gael had confidence enough to share with them all. Even before the scheduled hour was over, other reporters were calling to beg interviews. It wasn't until midnight that the Scouts were able to settle down in the luxurious but temporary quarters that Artveldt Construction had built in the base of the Statue of Liberty. They tumbled into bed and fell instantly asleep.

It was just past three in the morning when Royd came awake, aware of Gael and Iris in their uniforms above him. "What's happening?" he asked.

"Tovi just called," Gael answered. "Stinky went right to De' Big. Tovi wants us to meet her there."

He sat up, reaching for his uniform. It was pleasantly warm as he pulled it on. "Shouldn't we call the Police? And Jav?"

"Not…yet."

Suddenly Royd was fully awake. "Why not?"

"Tovi called from...the Artveldt Enterprises offices."
He nodded. "Let's go."

❖

Tovi met them in the lobby, all but transparent and obviously ill-at-ease amid the splendor of Artveldt Enterprises gilt and marble. After listening to her story, the teens knew at once that there was only one course of action.

Gael thumbed on her comm unit. "Get me De' Colleen Artveldt," she commanded.

De' Artveldt answered at once. "Gael, you ought to be asleep. What can I do for you?"

"We need to see you right away."

"Of course. I'm in my office. Come right up."

"Are you alone?"

"As it happens, yes. The staff is all busy at the moment."

"Good. We're on our way."

De' Artveldt met them at the door and ushered them in. She looked pointedly at Tovi, who had firmed up a little but was still translucent. "Who's your friend?"

"Tovi Witzell," Gael said. "She helped us settle the gang war this afternoon."

Royd forced a smile. "If we can convince her, she's going to become a PsiScout. And bring Omicron Force into the Youth Corps, too."

"Excellent." De' Artveldt frowned. "But that's not what you came up here for, is it?"

"No," Gael admitted. "De' Artveldt, is Stan Lovan here tonight?"

"Yes, he's up to his elbows in seed futures."

"Could you call him in, please? It's important."

De' Artveldt held Gael in her gaze for a moment, then nodded and raised her eyes. "Stan, would you come to my office?"

"Colleen, I'm in the middle of—"

"Yes, I know. Drop it and come in here."

They heard his sigh. "All right."

Seconds later, the door opened and he stepped in. Royd moved behind him, blocking the door.

"Is that the man?" Gael asked Tovi.

Tovi nodded. "That's him."

Lovan glared at Gael. "Colleen, what the hell is going on here?"

"That's what I'd like to know," De' Artveldt said. "Kids, what's this about?"

"De' Lovan is the Earthside leader of the Triton Liberation Front," Gael said.

Lovan laughed. "I have never heard anything so ridiculous. Colleen, I've been patient with these children of yours, but this is going entirely too far!"

Artveldt cocked her head. "So you're not involved in the Triton—"

"Of course not. The idea is absurd."

"Then you won't mind if Mentaxa administers a mind probe?"

Lovan twisted, grabbing Gael and throwing her at De' Artveldt's desk. As Gael and Artveldt went down, Lovan rushed at Royd. As he came, he raised a small energy pistol.

The blast hit Royd in the chest, and he fell back against the door. He hardly felt the impact. His chest felt like it was on fire, but an amazed glance told him that his suit had deflected the worst of the beam. He was unhurt!

Lovan slammed up against him, crumpled to his knees, and turned to face De' Artveldt. He raised the pistol and fired once more.

The beam splattered harmlessly against De' Artveldt's side.

Help me, Mentaxa thoughtcast. *I need your strength to hold him.* She stood firm, feet apart, and fixed Lovan in her gaze. Slowly, he lowered the pistol and let it fall. *Yes. It is over. Go to sleep.*

Lovan closed his eyes and slumped to the floor.

❖

Mentaxa stood by while two Police telepaths probed Lovan's sleeping mind. Then, letting the Police take him away, she reported to the others over hot chocolate in De' Artveldt's office.

"He is the one who was trying to kill you," she told De' Artveldt. "That stunt with the remote-controlled truck was just to throw everyone off suspecting him."

"Why?"

Mentaxa lowered her head. "The Triton Liberation Front. You…recently canceled some sort of deal that would have given them a lot of money."

"I found out they were fronting a company we traded heavily with. Our products were going right to Triton to be traded for arms. I pulled us out of the deal. The other company collapsed."

"After that, he knew you were on the lookout for a connection in Artveldt Enterprises. He thought that killing you was the only way to make you give up."

"He was probably right." She shook her head. "But I never suspected Stan." She shrugged. "Well, that's water under the bridge. I was a fool, and billions of my credits went to kill innocent people." She squeezed Iris's hand. "Thank the gods you kids came into my life at the right moment."

Royd yawned, doing his best to cover it up. De' Artveldt smiled wryly.

"It's late. You four have had a long and busy day. Don't head back to Liberty…use one of the suites downstairs. I think we all need to get some sleep."

Nodding, the teens drained their cups and said goodnight. Royd stumbled into the bedroom, slipped out of his suit, and fell into bed. He knew he would be asleep as soon as his head hit the pillow.

But in that last instant, before sleep closed around him, he was conscious of a final thought—not even sure if it was his own—*I wonder what tomorrow will be like?*

❖

Part Two:

The Case of the
Nucleus Jewel

ROLL CALL:
  Bolt
  Coloumb
  Fade
  Mentaxa

INTRODUCING:
  Colossus
  Legion
  Mimic

April AD 2574

EARTHNET alt.trends.commentary ON Mon Apr 25, 2574
Sec: 3 Thread: 1
FROM: pjenthen@artveldt.com [YouthCorps PR] AT 08:32:18
——————————

ATTENTION: All Puterpunks, Vidbrats, Netrunners, Drop-outs, Streetkids, Gangers, Bopts, Buddas, and Just Plain Kids!

Want to be part of something big? Want to learn to be your best? Want to belong? Then come join the most stellar club this side of U Orionis. The Youth Corps is for you!

The Irregulars take kiddos six through twelve. Teeners become full members. If you're in a gang, you don't have to worry about losing your buddos—in most cases, the Corps can co-opt your entire gang. We believe in keeping families together. Word.

We'll teach you what you need to know...and sib, it ain't stuff you learn in school.

If you think you belong in the Youth Corps, give us a buzz at recruiter@youthcorps.com. We'll give you the good news.

Doubleplus: if you're over twelve and have unusual psi Talents or other qualifying abilities, and if you think you have what it takes to be a Champion, then register for PsiScouts tryouts monthly at the Lady Named Liberty.

It's a new world, sib and cous, and we want you to be part of it. Let's hear from you.
——————————

❖

Fade walked along the shore, singing to herself. It was an old song, one her mother had sung when she was a little girl, long ago that she still had a home and a mother and a wonderful fluffy blanket to keep off the chill.

"Fade." She said her new name, let the wind take it and whirl it off to sea. Not Tovi Witzell any more; now she was Fade. Tovi had moved on, joined a new gang, left no forwarding netcode. The rich lady's people had given her new makeup and hairdo, a new white-and-black uniform, and a new name.

"Fade," she said, a little louder. Then, taking a great big breath, she threw her head back and shouted it: "Fade!" The word echoed from the nearby facets of the Manhattan dome, startling some seagulls into sudden and noisy flight.

Still not loud enough. No shout could be loud enough, not to bridge the gap between worlds and reach the ears of the mother who'd left her so many years ago.

Tyzgab was far away, far away in a direction that Fade couldn't begin to name, couldn't point to. Tyzgab existed in another dimension, a phantom world that sometimes—when the fog was heavy, or when summer stillness brought ripples to the air—sometimes touched Earth. Mirage, delusion, nightmare...so was Tyzgab known, on Earth.

And so was Earth known, on Tyzgab. Only the scientists were able to bridge the gap, to open commerce and communication between sister worlds a universe apart. Only scientists...and the occasional psionic mutant, like Fade.

She felt, now, the effort of staying in phase with Earth. Were she to relax, she would begin to drift back...to become intangible, invisible. And so Earth would become to her: a ghost of a world, no more real than a holoshow. Relaxing further, then, she could let go of Earth entirely, drift in the trackless wastes of the Shadow Domain...and come at last to home: Tyzgab. If she ever wanted to go home again.

Fade shook her head. No reason to go home. There she was nothing. Here she was a celebrity, a PsiScout. Here she had power.

Here she had a family.

Her communit beeped to signal an incoming message. "Fade, this is Bolt. Can you come to HQ right away? We have a case...for real."

"What's down?"

"Tell you when you get there, okay?"

"Suits." Fade reached to her back, unslung her jetboard and threw it toward the ground. The board quivered, then steadied ten centimeters above the ground. The frictionless clingfield would keep it at just that distance from dirt, street, or permaplast surface. She snapped her right foot into the stirrups, then pushed off with her left.

"Hey!"

Fade turned her torso, careful not to change the direction of the jetboard. Behind her, a teener boy in lavender and gold was waving frantically. "Stop!"

Fade braked, coming to rest a good twenty meters from the dome. She waited as the boy ran up to her. "You're Fade, of the PsiScouts, aren't you?"

"Who wants to know?"

The boy lowered his eyes. "I'm Lethim Barog of Garagk. I want to join your group."

"Hon, so do every punk onplanet. You got our netcode? Give a   buzz." The boy looked crestfallen, so Fade added, "Open house at Liberty next month, tryouts for new Scouts, big party. Buzz netcode, they tell ye."

"I want to be a Scout. I-I've got a really great Talent."

"What ye do special? Fly? Throw fire? See future?"

Lethim swallowed. "Take me in, let me demonstrate."

"Buddo, ye gotta buzz netcode, set up appointment. Do by rules, okay?"

He turned wide eyes on her. "I buzzed. They told me about tryouts next month. But I-I can't wait that long. I...don't think I'll be around then."

Fade dismounted and kicked her jetboard, which popped into her waiting hands. "Buckyboy, be ye in trouble?"

He nodded. "Big trouble. Bad trouble." He lowered his voice to a whisper. "Gang trouble. The kind of trouble that lands you at the bottom of the harbor."

Fade sighed. No one knew better than she that gang vendettas were deadly serious—and could spring up without warning and without real provocation.

Sometimes.

She wanted to ask Lethim what gang he was running from, what he'd done—but she held her tongue. That was Tovi Witzell's gig, not Fade's. PsiScouts didn't play gang politics.

PsiScouts helped people in trouble. Especially teeners.

She tossed down her jetboard and mounted again. "Ye can come. Up on board, hold tight."

His arms closed about her waist. Fade kicked off, then toed the switch that kicked in the jet-assist. At ten centimeters altitude, they shot off across the water toward Liberty Island.

❖

Coulomb was up to his ears in little kids.

It wasn't that he minded kiddos. He'd left a year-old brother on Taarla, and still counted the day Bren arrived as one of the happiest in his life. But one little brother was quite a bit different from fifty preteeners all going wild in one room.

He threw up his hands and shouted, "Everybody BE QUIET!" Silence fell, and fifty dirty faces with fifty pairs of eyes speared him. "All right, I have enough patches for everyone, but you're all going to have to line up. Uh... smallest kids in front. Everybody look at your neighbors; if you're shorter than anyone else, get in front of them."

"I'm the same size as him," one urchin protested.

Well, Coulomb reflected, he had asked for it. When De' Artveldt requested a volunteer to co-ordinate the newly-formed Youth Corps Irregulars, Coulomb had stepped forward before any of the others. Only now did he have second thoughts.

A young teener boy, ganger by the look of his precisely-tattered, ill-fitting clothes, came to the rescue. With a smile, he tapped the complaining kid on the head. "Since you two are the same size, you stand together, okay? Hold hands, right?" He winked at Coulomb, then raised his voice and said,

"Okay, kiddos, I want you all to look around and find somebody your own size. Hold hands and line up here."

"Thanks," Coulomb whispered.

"Nada problem," the boy said. He moved down the developing line of kiddos, moving them from one position to another like game pieces, all the while joking and wrestling with them. By the time he returned to Coulomb, the children were roughly lined up by height, and as well-behaved as excited pre-teeners could be. "What now, boss?" the boy asked.

Coulomb gestured to a box of Youth Corps patches. "Everybody gets a patch. Then we turn loose the teachrons." Artveldt Enterprises had provided the Corps with the most sophisticated AI programs available; through their patches, each kid would have a fulltime, holographic teachron to guide them through an individualized course of development. Teachrons could not solve all the problems of these at-risk kiddos, but they were certainly a start.

Once each kid had a patch, Coulomb announced, "Now we're going to activate your teachrons and give you some time to play with them. Then at noon we'll serve lunch."

All around the room, teachrons sprang into being—each a miniature version of Lady Liberty. Singly and in small groups, the kiddos drifted apart to start getting to know their teachrons.

The ganger boy, still smiling, said, "Isn't it kinda chancy to give these things out? The Educators' Union is going to hate your guts."

Coulomb shrugged. "The kiddos we're targeting are ones the Educators gave up on." He grinned. "We have other plans for kids in school."

There was a moment of silence, then the boy said, "Oh, well...is there anything else I can do to help?"

"I don't know. Hey, thanks for stepping in like that. You're really good with kids. I'm sorry, I didn't even get your name."

"Lethim. Lethim Barog." They shook hands.

"I can give you a patch if you want," Coulomb offered. "But you seem a little old for the Irregulars."

"I'm thirteen." Lethim looked away. "I...uh, what I really want is to be a PsiScout."

Coulomb swallowed. "Umm...Scouts have to have psi abilities of some kind. But we need a lot of teeners to help us with—"

"I have a psi talent."

"What? Oh, great! 'Course, that doesn't guarantee that you'll be accepted. We haven't—" The breep of his communit interrupted Royd, signaling an official message. "Hold on a second. Duty calls." He stepped away from Lethim and answered, "Coulomb here."

"Cou, this is Bolt. Can you come to HQ right away?"

A chill scampered down his spine. A real case! "Sure. Be right there. Out." He turned back to Lethim, who was politely looking elsewhere. "I've got to get into HQ."

"Oh. Well, I guess I'll—"

"You're coming with me. We can talk about it when we get there. Have you ever ridden tandem on a jetboard?"

"Sure."

"Then what are you standing there for? Come on."

❖

The dead surrounded Mentaxa, nearly a thousand years of them altogether. She sat quietly atop a weathered, partly-overgrown monument, her legs crossed and her mind at peace as she contemplated the dead.

This little graveyard, tucked away in a sleepy corner of the bustling city, had already become one of Mentaxa's favorite retreats. Perhaps it was the shady trees, or the stillness of the cool air, or the dead themselves insulating her from the pressure of too many living minds—Mentaxa felt calmer here than anywhere else she'd found.

She had learned a lot in the past week—they all had. Only here in the graveyard, relaxed, did she fully realize how much of an effort it was just to walk around sane in a city of so many unshielded minds.

On Ceres, in the Telepathic Institute, all inhabitants knew how to shield their minds, to keep thoughts and emotions from spilling out and splashing passersby. Here on Earth, no one shielded their minds—which just meant that Mentaxa had to erect barriers around herself, shields to keep out Earth's raging cacophony. And on the whole, she had been very successful. Still, at times she had to find some escape, some solace.

That was when she came to the graveyard.

Mentaxa stretched, and felt the city—and the world—around her. With her subconscious shields up, she sensed only a gentle susurrus, like the languid voice of distant surf. Easy to grow accustomed to, easy to ignore.

When she concentrated just a bit more, she picked up the mental signatures of those she knew well. There was Bolt, and there Coulomb: at the fringes of her awareness, so close that only the slightest effort would serve to pull them into rapport.

Slightly more distant, bright stars in a cold midwinter sky, she sensed Fade, De' Artveldt, Jav, and a handful of other friends. There, too, were her best teachers at the Institute, only a thought away. Beyond them, in endless and ever-changing constellations, were the massed minds of the city and the world, fading with physical and social distance.

Mentaxa felt a sharp stab, brought up her mental shields, and looked around. Yes—someone else had entered the graveyard. A boy, about her own age: a little chubby, dirty blond, wearing nondescript clothes in subdued orange and purple. Some gang's colors, she thought. On his head was a matching headband. His face and hands were the color of sand.

Mentaxa nodded to the interloper, then turned away. He had just as much right to use the graveyard as she did, and he deserved his privacy. She remained aware of him, though, aware of his casual stroll and his meandering progress among the graves—but most of all, she was aware of his unwavering gaze, his close attention upon her. She sensed no hostility, nothing to be alarmed at…just that he kept watching her.

She stood it until she felt him only two meters behind her, then spun. "All right," she demanded, "Who are you and what do you want?"

The boy backed away a step, arms raised. "I mean no harm."

The surface layers of his mind said he was telling the truth, and Mentaxa didn't want to move any deeper without good reason. Reading minds was hard work…in addition to being an invasion of privacy. The Institute had taught her well to take responsibility for her powers.

"Why are you stalking me?"

"I'm not stalking!" The boy took an embarrassed breath. "My name is Lethim Barog, and I want to be a PsiScout."

Mentaxa was on the verge of a snappy rejoinder when her communit signaled. "Bolt here. Mentaxa, please come to HQ. We have a case."

For an instant Mentaxa was torn between her annoyance at the boy, and Bolt's enthusiasm flooding the rapport-linked basement of her mind. Then she caught the undercurrent of seriousness in Bolt's emotions—this case was for real.

She thoughtcast, *Bolt, do you think this is going to be a difficult one?*

I think we'll need all the help we can get, Bolt replied.

Good. Maybe I have someone. See you soon. She gave the boy a slight nod. "All right, come on. I will take you to HQ for a tryout. But I do not make any promises."

"Huh?"

"Better get some new ear implants. I said come with me. If you pass, you are in."

❖

A crowd of curious onlookers nearly blocked the entrance to HQ. Fade relaxed her control enough to become immaterial and semi-transparent, and moved forward through the crowd, leaving Lethim to follow her as best he could. The crowd, of course, loved her performance: as she moved, people kept waving their hands through her with delight.

At the door, Fade waited for Lethim, expecting that the security program would stop him until she introduced him. Instead, as they crossed the threshold, Security whispered its usual confirmation in her ear: "Admitting PsiScout Fade and cleared visitor Lethim Barog."

"Acknowledged," she replied. To Lethim, she said, "That your power? Mess with computers' heads?"

The boy smiled and shook his head. "You'll see."

Fade shrugged, solidified, and stepped into the central dropshaft. The floor fell away from her as she shot upward, past still-empty levels to Liberty's crown in ten seconds. An instant later, Lethim popped up beside her.

The others were waiting at the conference table, which stood before a large viewscreen. Currently the screen showed a panoramic view of the harbor. Fade took a step forward, then stopped. Behind her, Lethim Barog laughed.

There was Bolt, Coulomb and Mentaxa, their friend Jav, Zhene Carmody from Artveldt Enterprises, another 'dult she didn't recognize...and Lethim Barog. Two of him, in fact. With the one behind her, that made three. All in identical clothes.

She faced the boy behind her. "You're triplets," she guessed.

He shook his head. "Try again."

Bolt stood up. "All right, what is this all ab— "

Where three Lethim Barogs had stood, now there six...all grinning like fools. Then, one by one, like soap bubbles popping, they disappeared until only one was left.

Fade realized that her mouth was hanging open, closed it. Bolt sputtered, Mentaxa smiled, and Coulomb said, "Okay, how'd you do that?"

Lethim shrugged. "I'm psi-gifted," he said. "They tell me it's just like astral projection, except my astral bodies are real. I can do up to six at a time."

Fade saw Jav's ears perk up—here was a story! But he'd promised not to go public with anything he learned from the PsiScouts without everyone's agreement. Still, she could tell he was itching to switch on a drone and start an interview right then and there. "Six bodies...all identical?"

"Near as I can tell. My clothes get duplicated to. I've been written up in med journals. I can give you the article citations if you want."

"Never mind, I can get 'em. Uh...what does it feel like? Which one is the *real* you?"

Lethim spread his hands. "All my selves are independent. When they merge, I remember everything that they all experienced. There's no special 'real' me."

Bolt glanced from Coulomb to Mentaxa to Fade. "Tell you what. Lethim, you've got a pretty impressive Talent. We can give you a trial period, and if you pass you're in. Unless anyone has any objections...?"

The 'dult, a bulge-muscled man with a disapproving scowl and the general air of a cop, piped up with, "You ought to at least run a security check before you allow someone into your organization."

Fade bit back a reply. She saw Bolt take a deep breath, then fix a smile.

"We're always grateful for the advice of the Earth Police, Officer Ran. Thank you." She turned to Lethim. "I'm sorry about this, Lethim. I completely forgot that our bylaws require that all membership matters be discussed in closed meetings. I shouldn't have brought it up when we have guests." She gestured to an empty seat next to her. "Come, sit down here, and when the briefing is over we can reopen the question. It won't be long."

Fade stifled a grin. Being polite like this was killing Bolt.

As Lethim and Fade took their seats, Bolt nodded to De' Carmody. "Zhene, will you get us started?"

Fade had discovered that there were two kinds of 'dults. The first kind did everything in their power to prevent kids from doing what they wanted. The second kind went out of their way to help kids do what they wanted.

Zhene Carmody was the second kind of 'dult...smart, precise, and young enough that she still remembered what it was like to be a teener. Of course, the fact that she was shorter than Coulomb, and had only a few centimeters on Bolt, didn't hurt either.

She stood up, holding a datapad casually but without referring to it. "This is Officer Ki Ran of the Earth Police Diplomatic Corps. He's come to us with a major problem; Chief Ormandeau thinks that the PsiScouts may be able to help. First, I'd like to give you a little background."

Zhene touched her pad, and on the big viewscreen the harbor faded to monochrome, while a holographic image appeared in full color. At first Fade thought the holo showed a planet from space; then she saw that the "planet" rested in the palm of someone's hand, and realized it was a perfectly-round, highly-polished stone of swirling white and blues.

"This is the Nucleus Jewel," Zhene said. "Found by an archeological team on Borath III about six years ago. Since then, it's been in the Smithsonian. Until yesterday."

Mentaxa, stone-faced, said, "As I remember, the currently-accepted theory has that the Nucleus Jewel is some kind of data-storage lattice left over from the Late Urtok Empire. One fellow claimed to have discovered how to decipher it, but I never heard any follow-up."

"How did you know that?" Officer Ran looked surprised, and Fade caught Jav trying to hide a smile.

"It is my job to know," Mentaxa answered.

Zhene moved in smoothly and quickly. "Yesterday the Nucleus Jewel disappeared from the Smithsonian."

"And you want us to find out who stole it?" Coulomb interrupted.

Officer Ran snorted. "We *know* who stole it. We know who has it now."

"So what do you want us to do?"

The man sighed. "Officially, nothing at all. Unofficially, we want you…to get it back for us."

Bolt leaned forward. "Officer, I think you'd better start at the beginning."

"The Chilpan Ambassador has the Nucleus Jewel," Officer Ran said.

Zhene elaborated. "Chilpan is an independent cluster of planets out on the March. It's a haven for smugglers, pirates, and general disreputable characters." She smiled. "Your kind of people, Fade."

"Our sources," the policeman continued, "Told us that the Jewel arrived at the Chilpan Embassy last night. As far as we can tell, it hasn't left."

Coulomb's brow wrinkled. "I guess this is a stupid question…but since you know where it is, why can't you get a…whatchacallit?…search warrant, and just go in and get it?"

Officer Ran groaned, and Bolt said, "No, you can't do that, not with an Embassy. See, it's like the Embassy is Chilpan territory. An Earth search warrant doesn't apply. If the Police enter, it's just like Earth invading Chilpan."

"Okay, but can't the Myriad Worlds—?"

Jav shook his head. "Chilpan isn't a member."

Coulomb frowned. "All right, I suppose that makes sense. It's stupid, though."

Bolt leveled her eyes on Officer Ran. "So what exactly do you want us to do? Break in and steal the Jewel back?"

Ran held up his hands, signaling that he didn't want to hear. "The Police don't care what you do. We don't want to know what you plan to do. Breaking into the Chilpan

Embassy would be illegal, and could very well start an interstellar incident." He glanced at his wrist, then stood up. "It's late. I'd better be going."

Coulomb opened his mouth, then closed it again at a glance from Mentaxa. Officer Ran strode to the dropshaft and fell out of   sight. A moment later, Security whispered in Fade's ear, "Earth Police Officer Ki Ran departing."

"Acknowledged," Bolt answered. "Well, boys and girls, it looks like we have a situation here."

Fade snorted. "Some situation. Police tell us, raid Chilpan Embassy. But if get caught, no, no, naughty teeners broke law. Throw 'em in jail, send to rehab. Make example."

Zhene shook her head. "No one's going to jail. Chief Ormandeau assured me of that." She pursed her lips. "Still, you're going to have to be careful, because if the Police catch you, they'll take some action. Probably a stiff fine. Not that Colleen can't afford it."

Mentaxa looked up. "And what if Chilpan catches us?"

Zhene had no answer.

❖

For the sake of formality, Jav and Zhene stepped out of the room while the PsiScouts "discussed" Lethim's membership. Approving him for a trial period was easy—"But he only gets one vote," Coulomb insisted. Then Jav and Zhene rejoined them for   the more difficult task: picking a code name for Lethim.

They spent half an hour debating a dozen suggestions, including "Replikon," "Multiplex," and Bolt's favorite, "Split Infinitive." Then Mentaxa, who had remained quiet, said softly, "Why do we not ask Zhene to query Artveldt Public Relations? They get paid for this sort of thing."

In less than an hour, Penna Jenthen's PR team had Lethim decked out in a new costume—of subdued purple and tan—and a new name: Legion.

De' Jenthen herself, a willowy, rather frantic woman, came to PsiScouts Headquarters to deliver the new costume. She assembled everyone in the lounge and insisted on fitting Lethim's accessories properly. Halfway through, she stopped. "Oh my god, what happens when you split? Are your other selves going to turn out naked?"

Lethim laughed. "Usually, my clothes multiply along with me. Let's see." His body blurred for an instant, then two Lethims stood there, both in identical PsiScouts outfits.

Zhene leaned forward. "Fascinating. Do both comm units work?"

Obediently, the Lethims took turns trying their comm circuits, then nodded and said in unison, "They seem to."

"Onboard computer? Net hookups? Pressure gear?"

"Everything works."

Zhene shook her head. "You kids are really something. Lethim, do you realize that you're breaking the Law of Conservation of Energy? You can't just go around creating sophisticated outfits like that out of thin air—"

The Lethims collapsed into one. "I didn't create anything. At least, nothing permanent."

"B-but…it defies belief."

Bolt put her hand on Zhene's shoulder. "Seems to me that once you believe a boy can split into six identical duplicates, you pretty much have to agree that a few extra costumes are no big deal."

"Nice costume, too." Lethim raised his arms and turned around, admiring his own reflection. "I think I'm going to like it here."

De' Jenthen fussed with his hair. "First, we'll send out a release announcing that there's a new PsiScout."

"Hey," Jav grumbled, "I get to announce first."

"Of course! We've been directing fans to your SIG for the most up-to-date PsiScouts coverage going. You'll run the announcement and do the first public interview with Legion." She frowned, gnawed at a fingernail, then brightened. "I know. How about a series of full-bandwidth clips showing our new Scout dashing off into action on his first case? The hint of danger, the uncertainty—but with artsy, sentimental touches. Sort of a wistful, my-little-boy-grows-up combined with so-proud-of-you, to grab 'em by the parental instincts."

Lethim rolled his eyes while the other PsiScouts laughed. De' Jenthen joined the laughter. "I'm sorry, Legion, I didn't mean to embarrass you. We'll keep the shooting short. Most of the effect will be in backgrounds and subliminals."

Fade jabbed Lethim with her elbow. "Little boy grows up," she giggled.

"Oh, we'll do the 'my little girl' versions of that spot as well," Penna said. Fade froze, glaring.

Before Fade could answer, Bolt stepped in. "De' Jenthen, I don't know how we'd manage without you. Colleen ought to give you a raise."

"I don't mind, honestly I don't." She dropped her voice to a conspiratorial whisper. "This is so much more fun than what I usually have to work on. That's why I steal all your assignments for myself." A breep interrupted her and she glanced at her wrist. "Look at the time! I have an appointment with Maintenance." She started toward the dropshaft. "Tell you what, Legion, I'll book a time to film that spot. And the rest of you, too. We have to—" The rest of her sentence was cut off as she dropped out of sight.

Zhene stared after her. "That woman wears me out." She sighed. "So have you decided what you're going to do about the Nucleus Jewel?"

"I have a few ideas," Bolt said. "But I'd like to hear what everyone else thinks first."

Fade, pulling a bottle of nemo-juice out of stasis, cocked her head. "Fade out, sneak in, grab Jewel." She shrugged her shoulders. "Simple."

Mentaxa looked icicles in her direction. "You cannot make the Jewel iteself invisible, can you?"

Fade grinned. "Could try. Tuck it under jacket. What, ye think they'd notice if Nucleus Jewel decides to take a stroll?"

Coulomb cleared his throat. "I think the first problem is to make sure that no one leaves the Embassy with the Jewel. Then we need to find out exactly where it is, get in, and get out—all undetected."

"Is that all?" Lethim chuckled. "We should be finished by this afternoon. Time for a show. Hey, Fade, toss me one of those juices, eh?"

"All kidding aside," Bolt said, "Cou is right. Let's take it one step at a time. How do we make sure nobody takes the Jewel out of the Embassy?"

Mentaxa leaned back, steepling her fingers. "While the rest of you were planning how to hype our new member, I was on the nets doing some research. Officer Friendly was right: the cops cannot enter the Embassy, touch any of the diplomats, or inspect any official packages going in or out."

"We're sunk." Coulomb threw up his hands. "They'll just send the Jewel back to Chilpan. It's probably on its way already."

"In actual fact," Mentaxa continued, "There are some things the cops *are* allowed to do, and so far they've done them just right." She ticked off on her fingers. "They have put a security cordon around the Embassy, keeping citizens away. They have restricted all vehicular traffic in the area. Any movement in or out is going to be very obvious. In addition, the cops have made it known that if the Jewel heads for the spaceport, then the ship that carries it will find pirates waiting for them when they clear Earthspace."

Jav frowned. "I've got a dæmon watching the cops' public nets, and they're getting a lot of flack for the traffic shutdown. From everywhere, not just Chilpan. They won't be able to keep the cordon in effect for more than a few hours longer."

"Then we need to act pretty quickly," Bolt said. "Fade, what about the Irregulars? What gangers do we have in the area?"

Fade thought. "Embassy Row. That be Turboflash territory. Executor, Red Sector treaty partners. Can call on all three."

"How's this: Bring all the gangers into the area. Make it obvious that they're hanging around. Get the cops to stay off their backs. Stage a Turboflash block party. Invite other friendly gangs."

Legion grinned. "I don't know any 'dult who'd feel comfortable going out in that."

Zhene nodded. "That should keep them penned up in the Embassy. Especially if we spread the word that our gangers will be actively looking for the Jewel to be smuggled out."

"And if Officer Friendly will keep the cops away."

"I think he'll co-operate. That still leaves the problem of how to get to the Jewel."

"Been thinkin'," Fade said. "Somebody in there oughta have that Jewel on their mind. Oughta be keepin' an eye on it, thinkin' about where it is, is it safe, how much it worth, all that. Our Mentaxa reads minds."

Mentaxa considered. "If I can get close enough...I should be able to do it."

"Fine, then," Bolt said. "Fade, get in touch with Turboflash and the other gangers. Zhene, will you tell Officer Ran what we're up to? As soon as the gangs get going, we'll move in and see if Mentaxa can pick up anything. Everbody okay with that? Good. Let's go."

❖

There was nothing in the world to compare with a ganger block party. Here was music, roaring from a dozen different blare-boxes, filling the air with a wild syncopation of beats guaranteed to drive 'dults mad. Here was food, a junkfood smorgasbord from all around the world, set up on makeshift tables or passed hand-to-hand through the crowd. Here was dancing, and flirting, and singing, and bragging, and running, and giggling, and all the other things that kids do together.

Most of all, here were kids: teeners, kiddos, even some tods under the care of older sibs. Brown kids, yellow kids, pink kids, blue kids—kids painted in dayglo tiger-stripes and iridescent   leopard-spots, every shade of the spectrum. Turboflash cheek tattoos predominated, but Fade saw markings and colors from gangs as far away as Antarctica and Luna Farside. And more arriving every second.

Four thousand kids jammed the area around Embassy Row, bringing traffic and business to a complete halt while they partied. Four thousand kids in an area six blocks by three, and more pouring in, responding to the call of similarity and the appeal of a wild bash.

Four thousand kids…yet there was not a single fight. The PsiScouts roamed the streets, half-ready for trouble that didn't materialize. After about fifteen minutes, Bolt said, "The gangers are being well-behaved. I'm surprised."

Fade made the quick, two-handed gesture that throughout the galaxy meant the end to combat. "Truce," Fade said. "No fightin' allowed in Turboflash turf today. Anybody try it, they in deep karg. Outcast from gang, better not find theirself in dark alley at night." She shook her head. "Truce sacred."

As the PsiScouts strolled, ganger kids scuttled out of their way, or shouted greetings. Everyone, it seemed, had a good word, a smile, a wave for them.

"Damn," Mentaxa muttered, "We are popular. Who would have thought it?"

"You're kidding, right?" Legion replied. "The PsiScouts are the hottest thing in the Solar System right now. Most of these kids would throw themselves underneath a spaceship at liftoff if you asked them to."

"Truth?" Bolt asked.

"Truth!" Legion crossed his heart. "The 'dults may not know that much about you, but to kids you're the greatest."

"Don't get a swelled head now, Gael," Coulomb said.

"Jav would be thrilled." In order to avoid drawing attention to the Chilpan Embassy, Jav was at the spaceport covering a completely different story.

They had reached the Chilpan Embassy, an imposing ten-story building of ancient concrete-and-glass set back from the street and surrounded by a tall ornamental hedge. Fade thought she saw a few curious faces peering out of upper windows, but she couldn't be sure and didn't want to look too closely.

"So, Mentaxa, what do you think?" Bolt asked.

Mentaxa's eyes were closed and Coulomb was guiding her with a hand on her elbow. "I am trying to concentrate," she hissed. After a moment, she shook her head. "It is no good. Too much interference."

"You can do it, Iris." Bolt steered her toward a curb. "Here, sit down. We'll help you."

The three founding members—Bolt, Coulomb, and Mentaxa—joined hands and closed their eyes. Fade waved a couple of Turboflash gangers over and instructed them to stand between the Embassy and the Scouts. Other kids gathered naturally. With luck, the folks inside the Embassy wouldn't have any idea what was going on.

"All right," Mentaxa said, "I am getting something. They are...uneasy. Frightened." She opened unseeing eyes. "They are afraid of the gangers. Do not know what is happening. They...feel trapped."

"What about the Nucleus Jewel?" Bolt prompted.

Mentaxa closed her eyes again. "I am working on it. There is a feeling of...yes, there it is! Concern. Anxiety. Someone is thinking of the Jewel. Is it safe? The cops are gone, but now these crazy kids, who knows what they want?" Mentaxa's voice deepened. "I'll tell you one thing, Cremen Tag can't get here too soon for me. Do you think he'll fool the cops? Ha! Earth Police are stupider than icicle rats in the summertime. The Jewel will be offplanet before they even know it's missing."

"Mentaxa? Come on back, hon."

Mentaxa lowered her head, then pulled her hands away from Bolt and Coulomb and rubbed her eyes. "I am back. The Nucleus Jewel is still there, all right. On one of the top floors. Someone was looking out a window at us."

"At us?" Legion sounded worried.

"Not at us in particular. At the street." Mentaxa turned and regarded the building. "Probably the top floor. Let me think —it was a corner room. Windows on the right as well as in front. That means...it ought to be *that* room."

"Who's this Cremen Tag they're waiting for?"

Mentaxa frowned. "I do not know exactly. All I know is that they expect her—or him—to take the Jewel and get it safely offplanet. I sensed something about tunnels, or...I am not sure."

Legion nodded. "This whole area is crisscrossed with old sewer drains, inspection tunnels, accessways, who knows what all." He gestured to the inner surface of the dome, only a few dozen meters above the roofs of Embassy Row as it curved down into the East River a few blocks beyond. "Whenever you get near the edge of the dome, the ground is honeycombed."

Fade looked past the PsiScouts and grimaced. "Here come trouble."

The lanky boy who approached, wearing an Earth Police Cadet uniform, looked about as graceful as a Saint Bernard puppy—and, Fade thought, about as handsome too. His hands and feet were too big, and his ears stuck out like twin radar dishes scanning the path in front of him. His long, stringy hair gave him an unkempt, shaggy look. She wondered if he smelled like a dog.

"PsiScouts. Pleased to meet you." He stuck out his hand, then stood there grinning like an idiot when no one took it. "I understand you're trying to get the Nucleus Jewel back."

"Shhhh!" Bolt grabbed him high and Fade grabbed him low, and together they dragged him behind a lamppost. It offered scant cover from the Embassy, but anything was better than letting him stand out in the open blabbing. Mentaxa, Coulomb, and Legion gathered around, so the newcomer wound up against the pole surrounded by the Scouts.

"Who the karg are you and what are you talking about?" Bolt demanded.

The kid seemed unfazed. "I'm Gery Allin. The news is all over the precinct, that Chief Ormandeau asked the PsiScouts to get back the Nucleus Jewel. So I figured I'd come help you."

Fade snorted. "Cops! Can't keep anything secret."

Three others tried to talk all at once, and Bolt shushed them all with a minor thunderbolt. "Look, Gery, we'd really appreciate it if you didn't spread this around. See, we're trying to—"

"That's what I'm here for. To help you."

Mentaxa buried her face in her hands.

"I came to help you get back the Jewel," Gery continued, unfazed. "I figure, what you need is a diversion. While they're occupied, you can sneak in and get the Jewel out."

"That isn't exactly—"

"I'm great at diversions."

"I'm sure you are."

"No, really." The boy shrugged. "Or we don't have to do it that way. Just tell me what you want done, I'm your man."

Bolt took a deep breath. "Gery, what we need most for you to do is back off. It's bad enough that we've drawn attention to ourselves—"

"Wearing these costumes," Mentaxa said drily, "How could we not draw attention?"

"— But now the people in there have seen us talking to the EP's. They have to know something's up."

"Bottomline," Fade said, "Is: get lost, boyo."

Legion put his hand on Gery's shoulder. "Fade, that isn't very nice. How about if Gery's our liaison to the cops? Better him than Officer Friendly, right?"

Gery shrugged off his hand. "Never mind. I'll go ahead and get lost. You don't have to worry about me butting in on your hero game." With his lips drawn, Gery strode away.

Bolt let out her breath. "I didn't handle that very well."

"None of us did," Legion answered.

Fade tossed her hair in the direction of Gery's departing form. "G'riddance," she said.

"If you do not mind," Mentaxa said, "Can we decide what we are going to do about the Nucleus Jewel?"

"I'm fresh out of ideas," Bolt said.

Coulomb, brow furrowed, said, "Follow me." He led them across the street and down a block away from the Embassy, toward the water. The block party was in full swing down here, and Fade felt her suit's communit tie in so she could hear the others over the din of music and voices.

"They're going to take the Jewel out of there tonight, right?" Coulomb asked.

"As near as I can tell," Mentaxa answered.

"And they're going through some tunnels or under-ground passageways?"

"Yes. Cou, what are you getting at?"

"Why don't we set up a trap for them? Legion said the tunnels around here all go to the edge of the dome. I checked the city databanks, and there are maps of all the accessways. What if we lay out proximity detectors in each of the tunnels? Shouldn't be too hard to figure out where they're going and be waiting for them when they get there."

Bolt pursed her lips. "I don't know. Are you sure those old maps are right? I'd hate to—"

A wave of sound, like the crash of surf on a shore, stopped her. It came from behind them, from the Embassy, drowning out the music for an instant. Then, it resolved into the sound of hundreds of voices, all shouting.

"What's going on?"

Instantly, jetboards were out and the five PsiScouts, as a unit, sailed toward the Embassy.

The crowds, amazed, pushed back from the Embassy building. When Fade saw why, she stopped, frozen in disbelief.

Gery Allin, standing nearly twenty-five meters tall, stood on the Chilpan Embassy's lawn peering into a top-floor window.

Bolt groaned. "Someone please tell me that this is not happening."

Fade laughed. "Surprise! Cop cadet's a big boy."

"He's trying to find the Nucleus Jewel," Legion observed, as the giant-size Gery peered into one window after another.

Bolt's hair rose, surrounding her head with a red-gold nimbus. "He can't do this! If the Chilpani don't kill him, then his EP bosses will fry his hide for trespassing on an Embassy."

"What should we do, boss?" Coulomb asked.

"Snipers!" Mentaxa pointed at the Embassy. Armed troops appeared at the top windows, rifles aimed at Gery.

"Get that fool away from there!" Bolt commanded. "Coulomb, Legion, draw their fire. Your suits will protect you. Fade, try to get his attention. Mentaxa—"

"I am trying. I need to concentrate."

"Fine. Keep at it."

Coulomb sprang to his jetboard, skimmed the hedge and dropped to the lawn of the Embassy. At the same time, Legion split into six; each of his bodies went in a different direction as they raced onto the grounds.

Fade passed through the hedge and, keeping herself carefully intangible, approached Gery's enormous left foot. Overhead, blaster bolts struck Gery; he stumbled back a step, then steadied himself with an upraised hand against the dome.

"They're using stunners," Coulomb said over the comm. "And they aren't hurting him."

"Hey!" Fade shouted, waving, but Gery didn't hear her. She solidified, joined her hands, and threw a punch against his ankle. It was like hitting a steel wall...and he still didn't notice her.

"Skin like armor," she said.

"That makes sense," Coulomb answered, grunting as a stunner bolt hit him and splashed harmlessly against his suit. "To support him at that size, he'd need a pretty strong exoskeleton. I'll bet it's some kind of psionic force field."

"I cannot believe that you two are calmly discussing the physics of the situation," Bolt said.

"If ye want Big Boy to pay attention, we gonna have to hit with something big," Fade answered.

"Right. Phase out, then—something big is coming up."

Fade stepped back, relaxing until she was less substantial than a breath. Beyond the hedge, Bolt crouched to the ground, waving her hands as if feeling for something.

"Damn," Fade heard her swear, "There's got to be a power conduit around her somewhere."

"Back up!" Fade cried out. "Bolt's gonna throw lightning."

A second later, Bolt did throw lightning. She stood up, gestured at Gery, and eye-searing energy leapt from the ground at her feet, hitting Gery just below his right shoulder. He turned to look.

"Get the karg away from there!" Bolt yelled.

"He can't hear," Fade said.

The distraction, though, was enough. Five Chilpani snipers aimed, and their stunbeams converged on Gery's left temple. The giant stumbled, then fell—at the same time shrinking, until after a moment he was back to normal size, collapsed on the grass.

At once, the snipers concentrated their fire on Coulomb and Legion's six bodies. Fade saw a stunbeam pass, harmlessly, through her own body.

"Retreat," Bolt ordered. "Get off the Embassy grounds."

"What about Big Boy? Leave him?"

"I don't know."

"Right." Fade solidified, grabbed Gery and hoisted him to her back. He was taller than her but not as massy; she stumbled forward, aiming for the hedge.

She never got there. The first three stunbeams didn't penetrate her suit, but by the fourth shot the snipers were learning, and they joined fire. Fade felt a tingle, then her legs went out from beneath her and she crumpled.

❖

An hour later, the Turboflash block party was still going strong, although the street in front of the Chilpan Embassy remained empty. Fade, invisible and intangible, paused in the middle of the street while her comm unit located the other PsiScouts. Then, following the unit's directions, she moved through the crowd and toward the edge of the dome.

When the stunner had knocked her unconscious, her body had faded into the Shadow Domain, the in-between dimensional limbo that linked Tyzgab and Earth. Only when she regained consciousness was she able to phase back to Earth, invisible, in the spot where she'd fallen. Her suit told her it had been nearly an hour.

She'd quickly checked inside the Chilpan Embassy, then decided she'd better report to the others.

Behind her, the sun sank and the sky began to turn orange.

She found the others—Bolt, Mentaxa, Coulomb, and Legion—sitting on a concrete wall that overlooked a two-meter stretch of dirt and weeds; beyond that, a steep bank fell away to the river.

She firmed up her body, becoming visible again.

"Fade!" Coulomb cried. "We thought you'd been captured."

"An' ye thought they could hold me?"

"What can you report?" Bolt asked.

"I checked inside. Big Boy got hisself caught good. Cuffed in basement secure room. Complaining like old lady, making noises 'bout escape. Can't say I like that boy much, but he sure do got spunk." She nodded at Legion. "One o' ye other selfs there, too. Still knocked out. Told Big Boy I'd be back after I checked in."

They all looked at her funny, Bolt most of all. "You say Legion's there? Still unconscious?"

"One of 'im. Hey, we gotta get shields adjusted for stunners. Don' work too good."

Legion shook his head. "Fade...I'm not missing any of my bodies."

"What?"

He blurred, multiplied. "I'm all here." Sure enough, there were six of him.

"Then who the karg's in there? And what're we gonna do about it?"

"Hold on, Fade. There's something you have to see first." Bolt touched her wristpad, and Fade's comm unit signaled a recorded message.

The image blossomed in front of her, following the movements of her eyes. It was Officer Friendly...but he didn't look too friendly. His face was red, his lips tight.

"I trusted you kids, and you've made a big mess even worse. Now I have hostages to deal with, along with the Chilpan government filing complaints with my department." He glared. "I want you off this case. Go home and do nothing. That includes all your friends, as well. My officers are moving in at sundown, and if they find you in the area, I'm giving them orders to arrest you. Ran, out."

"You see?" Bolt said.

"What, ye're going to listen to him?"

"He's a Police Officer. We have to listen to him."

Fade chuckled. "Hon, ye got a lot t' learn. We told 'em we'd get their Jewel back, so we're gonna get it back. 'Sides, Big Boy up there is one of us—we can help him."

Coulomb nodded. "Gery is exactly the kind of at-risk kid we're supposed to be helping. What's going to happen to him if we just leave him?"

Legion grinned. "And I want to find out who's impersonating me."

Bolt sighed. "All right, all right, we'll do what we can. Mentaxa, did you get any idea when this Cremen Tag they're waiting for is going to arrive?"

"I got a vague feeling of 'later tonight.' After dark, I am sure. Nothing more exact."

"Okay, we'll go ahead with the plan of stopping them in the tunnels. Meanwhile, we need to rescue Gery—and whoever else is there. Fade, I need more information. Where are they being held? What can Gery do to help us? And who's the fellow who looks like Legion?"

"On my way."

❖

People in the Chilpan Embassy were very nervous as night fell. As Fade drifted through the building, she saw taut, drawn faces, readied guns, and more white knuckles than she could count.

Before going to the basement, she checked on the Nucleus Jewel. It had been moved from its upper-floor room, and was now locked in a safe in what she assumed was the Ambassador's office. Armed guards stood ready at the door.

Gery was straining futilely against his cuffs when she entered the sparsely-furnished basement room. Sitting on a chair beside him was…Legion. Even though she knew it wasn't him, she couldn't believe the resemblance. Hair, eyes, ears, everything was perfect, down to his orange-and-purple PsiScouts uniform.

Fade allowed herself to become visible and said, "Told ye I'd be back."

"Did you find the other PsiScouts? What did they say?"

"That ye've made a mess of things. And that we gotta get ye out." She turned to the Legion impostor. "Who ye be?"

He raised his eyes to her. "You know that Legion is not himself?"

"I know that ye ain't Legion. Speak."

"Do not be afraid." Legion stood up, shivered, and…began to melt.

Clothing and flesh flowed like melting wax, his form shrinking, losing color, changing. After half a minute, an entirely new creature stood before her: short, grey, with large ears, enormous eyes, and a great nose that was almost a snout. Its legs were thick and solid, and it had a stubby tail.

"Shapeshifter," Gery whispered.

"Tserifin hopes he did not startle you," the grey creature said. "Many people do not like shapeshifters."

"I've never seen one," Gery said.

"We do not often leave Homeworld."

Hands on hips, Fade demanded, "Tell me what ye do here, and why ye masquerade as Legion-boy."

"Tserifin meant no harm. He only wanted to help. He saw Gery Allin attack the Embassy, and he saw the PsiScouts try to stop Gery. He saw Chilpani guards shooting at Scouts. And Tserifin said to himself, 'They need help.' So Tserifin decided to look like Legion and get captured, in case he can help later."

Gery frowned. "And what were you doing outside the Embassy anyway?"

The little grey creature turned wide eyes on Fade. "Tserifin heard that the PsiScouts were going to be here. Tserifin wanted to see the Scouts. Tserifin wants to help them." He lowered his head. "Tserifin wishes to become a PsiScout."

He looked so helpless, and his voice was so plaintive, that Fade couldn't help a tender feeling toward the little guy. "How old ye be?"

"Tserifin is fourteen in Earth years. He left Homeworld in 2571, and has lived on Earth for eighteen months." Again the big eyes, wide and sad as the full Moon. "Tserifin has no friends and no family. He is lonely."

Gery gripped Tserifin's hand. "You have a friend now, buddy."

Fade shook her head. "Ye two make me sick." She sighed. "Okay, I'm a friend too. Now we talk—ye two are gonna help get Scouts out of this mess. Only thing is, how?"

"Tserifin has an idea…."

❖

Bolt wasn't happy, and she didn't see any way she could change the situation. The sky was red with sunset; any moment the Earth Police would be moving in to disperse the gangers. Fade had ordered the kids to take their time leaving, but not to resist…at most, the tactic would buy another half hour. Then the cops would want the PsiScouts gone. Or arrested.

Meanwhile, there was no sign of Cremen Tag coming to pick up the Nucleus Jewel. Coulomb, Mentaxa, and Legion had spread proximity detectors through all the tunnels that might lead to the Embassy—so far there's hadn't been so much as a squeak from the detectors.

"Calm down, boss," Legion said with his toothy smile. "It's up to Fade now. And Tserifin, whoever he is."

"I know," Bolt snapped. She forced herself to relax. "That's what I don't like—waiting out here without anything to do."

You are a control freak, Mentaxa thoughtcast, her mental voice conveying bored detachment. She and Coulomb were attempting to skip stones on the river; she threw one, then continued, *You need to feel that you are in charge. You go to pieces if you are not.*

In spite of herself, Bolt chuckled. *That's not really much of an insight, but thanks anyway.* She stretched, touched her toes, and tossed a stone. It fell with a single splash, far short of the inner surface of the dome.

Coulomb handed her another stone, lighter, flatter. "Here," he said, "Try again."

❖

The Chilpan Ambassador's office was isolated behind half-meter thick walls of duraplast composite. Nevertheless, those walls presented no more an obstacle to Fade than a steamy bathroom to anyone else. She drifted through, spotted the Ambassador at his desk, and took up position behind him. Her onboard computer silently signaled her that it had lost touch with the Nets; as she'd expected, the office was shielded.

The Ambassador was gruff-looking and bald, with drooping ears and pale yellow skin...all in all, a splendid specimen of a Chilpani businessman. His desk was a mess, covered with datascreens and micropads. Each one, it seemed, displayed something different—documents, datafeeds, various newsnets. She even caught a glimpse of Jav's face on one screen. Jav-boy'd be flattered, she thought, to know Ambassadors tracked his channel.

Tserifin had agreed to wait exactly five minutes; it had been four. Fade took a breath, then reached into the Ambassador's neck. As she allowed her hand to grow just barely solid, she felt a ghost of sensation, of warmth, a hint of texture. Her stomach lurched. This was worse than hiding within Stinky.

Grip, she told herself. Gritting her teeth, she moved her hands, stroking gathered nerves. It felt like touching wet spiderweb.

The Ambassador, unconscious at once, slowly tilted forward. Snatching her hand back, Fade solidified and caught him before his head hit the desk.

The next minute was endless. Fade worried that someone would call the Ambassador, or that a guard or secrebot would come through the door, or that the Ambassador wore medical telemeters that would sound an alert, or that —

A large black fly buzzed past her face, circled, then landed on the floor. Then the fly shimmered, expanded, flowed…and Tserifin took shape before her. "Tserifin found a way through where the data cables pierce the wall. He crawled through as a worm."

Fade cocked her head. "Where go mass, when ye become fly?"

"Tserifin does not understand," he whispered.

"Ye must mass fifty, fifty-five kilos. Fly masses half a gram. Where all the mass goes?"

Tserifin spread his arms. "Tserifin can answer that question in the language of Homeworld, but he does not have the words in Galangua. Mass and energy are same thing, no? Mind suspends energy." He shook his head. "It is a great effort, to become something as small as a worm or a fly. Much easier to become Human teenager or large dog."

"Ye can't make mass disappear!"

"Where does Fade's mass go, when she vanishes?"

Fade snorted. "I know right well where me mass go. Into Shadow Domain. Maybe ye send your mass there too." She shrugged. "We all be here. Be quiet now and I call Mentaxa."

She closed her eyes, trying to shut out the room, the Ambassador, the threat of the door opening any second. *Mentaxa,* she thought, *Fade here. Is time, girl!*

❖

Mentaxa looked up, catching Bolt's face perfectly silhouetted against a streetlight. The amber light drew patterns of gold in Bolt's hair. "I have just heard from Fade," she said. "Now is the time."

Bolt nodded. "Let's do it, kids."

Mentaxa joined hands with Bolt and Coulomb, while Legion split into six bodies and surrounded them, linking arms. Bolt's hand, and Coulomb's, felt like fire in her grip, and she realized that her own hands must be like ice to them. "Relax. Let your mind drift."

The Triad was easy: Mentaxa, Bolt, Coulomb, minds meshing as if they'd been born for one another, becoming almost one entity. Buoyed by Bolt's spirit, supported by Coulomb's steadiness, she reached out for Legion. For the Legions.

His mind—minds—were jumpy, frantic. "Grip, boy. Look at the water. Watch the waves. Relax. Do not try. Just be."

Ah, there it was. There *they* were, six minds nearly identical, bursting with energy and humor. Mentaxa took their strength and bound it into the Triad. It was as if the six Legions were lifting the three, raising them onto their sturdy shoulders in some gymnastic pyramid.

I could never do this on my own, Mentaxa thought, as she cast her mind outward, following the slender silver thread of thought that led her to Fade.

Mentaxa slipped into Fade's mind as she would slip into a set of pajamas. The fit was hardly perfect, the shape was all wrong...but with the power of the Triad supported by the Six, she could do it. Carefully, gently, she knitted Fade's mental processes into the gestalt.

Through Fade's eyes, she saw the short, grey form of Tserifin, the Ambassador unconscious at his desk, the walls and floor and ceiling that bounded this room. What Mentaxa was about to do, would never leave these walls.

Fade touched her hands to the Ambassador's temples, and Mentaxa touched her thoughts to his sleeping mind.

Slow, heavy, his memories beat in the alogical pattern of dreams. Mentaxa knew that she was working against a deadline, but she had to move ever so carefully—she traced line after line, the warp and weft of thought, then at the crucial moment inserted her own picture into the weave.

When the Ambassador awoke, he would not remember suddenly falling unconscious…instead, he would remember that he'd been yawning, that he was tired, that the room was so warm and the work before him so tedious, and before he'd known it, he'd fallen asleep.

Distantly, she heard a chuckle that she knew to be Legion's. He was enjoying this joke on the Ambassador.

A flavor of seriousness, drawn from Bolt's earnest concern, infused the gestalt minds. *Hurry.*

Mentaxa bent again to her task, tracing memories, nudging dreams first this way and then that, searching for images she needed. This was a gamble—they had no way of knowing if the Ambassador had ever seen Cremen Tag, or would know what recognition signals were expected. But it was a safe bet.

Yes…there. As if turning a corner onto an unexpected view, Mentaxa saw in the Ambassador's memory a picture of Cremen Tag. An unhealthy-looking man, Cremen Tag was: sallow skin, drooping eyes, parts of his face and body replaced by dull metallic cybimplants. The Ambassador needed little nudging; he was anxious about Cremen Tag's arrival, and played out the recognition signals in a quick dream-within-a-dream.

Mentaxa lifted her mental touch, preparing to leave the man's mind. There was only one thing left, a minor compulsion to plant. Again, it was easy, because the Ambassador was already anxious about his hostages, anxious about what the Earth Police would do. Anxious to be rid of both the Jewel and the hostages.

It only remained for Mentaxa to plant the simple suggestion, that Cremen Tag could rid him of both. Then, she withdrew completely from his mind. She had only to give the barest command, and the man would awake.

She allowed Fade to glance at her suit's time-display; three minutes was all her performance had taken. She lifted Fade's hands from the Ambassador's head, turned to Tserifin.

"Tserifin wonders if you are done," the creature said. "He wants you to know that he has felt nothing."

Hello, Tserifin, Mentaxa thoughtcast. *I am finished with him...now it is your turn.* When he drew back, she felt Fade smile. *Do not be afraid, this will not hurt a bit.*

"Tserifin isn't afraid. He just...." The moment of contact came, and Tserifin froze, his jaw hanging limp.

His mind was so strange, so different, so wonderful. Mentaxa felt as if she had stumbled into an enchanted forest, an undersea kingdom that had never known the touch of land, a whirling cloud of cosmic dust that would one day birth a new star. For a moment she could do nothing but look about in wonder, on the verge of losing herself in formlessness.

Focus, girl. That was Bolt again, dear practical action-oriented Bolt, dragging her back from the brink of wonder to remind her of the job that must be done. Breathing a silent "thank you," she proceeded.

Tserifin, here is what Cremen Tag looks like. And here is what he must do and say when he comes to the Embassy. Borrowed memories flowed, sank like water into dry sand. *Do you have it?*

Tserifin understands.

She pulled back, lingering for a moment in Fade's mind before allowing Fade's awareness to fall apart from the gestalt. In the back of her mind, she felt that the Legions were growing tense, that Bolt had a developing crick in her neck, that Coulomb's right foot was going to sleep, that her own body temperature was down almost to the point where her suit would start to scream for attention. None of them could maintain the gestalt much longer.

Do what you have to, now, she instructed Fade and Tserifin.

Fade, stepping back from the Ambassador, became invisible. Where Tserifin had stood, a lone fly now circled the room, then alighted on the wall and was gone.

Wake! She gave the order, then pulled back from Fade's mind entirely. The gestalt endured for a few seconds longer, as the last of the sun's light touched the clouds—then the sun was gone, and she let the Legions go. Then the Triad dissolved, and Mentaxa, cold and tired, tumbled to the ground.

❖

Tserifin knew he was lost, but he flew on. The Embassy's basement levels, which had looked so easy in the visual memories Mentaxa had transplanted from the Ambassador, were rather different through the eyes of a fly.

Walls were lost in the distance, signs hopelessly blurred beyond recognition, even color completely transformed. And everywhere he flew, every place he tried to light, Tserifin saw the living, moving mountains that were people. It wasn't safe anywhere.

After a minor eternity, Tserifin picked a particularly dark cavern—behind a piece of furniture, he guessed—and touched down at floor level. In another moment, he was a small, black mouse, and he realized he was hiding under a chair.

Cautiously, Tserifin poked his snout out from under the chair and surveyed the room. Two Chilpani sat nearby, engrossed in a video display; when he was sure he wouldn't be noticed, he skittered across the floor and into the main corridor.

As a mouse, he was just large enough to recognize features of the gargantuan landscape. He quickly found the stairway that led to the sub-basement access tunnels. No one was looking; he turned into a finch and took to the air, following the stairs downward. By the time he reached the bottom, he felt free to revert to his own form.

The sub-basement was dark and cramped with huge, thumming machinery. Behind a massive, two-hundred-year-old fusion reactor, Tserifin found a rusty, sealed hatch. Although it looked as if it had not been opened in decades, he knew that this was the primary route for the Embassy's illicit traffic. This was the hatch through which Cremen Tag would enter.

Not any more. The PsiScouts waiting outside would intercept the real Cremen Tag. Now, if only Mentaxa had transferred the right information....

Tserifin took a breath, then closed his eyes. Slowly, his flesh flowed, he grew taller and heavier, his facial features shifted. In a few moments, Tserifin was gone. In his place stood a perfect duplicate of Cremen Tag.

He reached for the hatch, then had to stop for a few seconds to steel his nerve. Tserifin had never tried such a detailed impersonation. He had virtually no idea of Cremen Tag's personality, how the man should behave. What if he made some mistake that tipped off the Ambassador?

Well, if Tserifin screwed up, then obviously Tserifin wasn't fit to be a PsiScout.

Confidence restored, he tugged at the release lever. It was rusty, but it moved fairly easily; the hatch swung open at once. Now it was go/nogo—the opened hatch would signal an alarm, someone would notify the Ambassador, and he would be down here demanding recognition signals.

Mentaxa, Tserifin is ready.

He hoped he wouldn't flub his lines.

❖

Fade struggled to pull on Legion's costume, then looked at her reflection in a darkened store window. She shook her head. "Ain't gonna work. They never believe I'm Legion-boy."

Coulomb thrust a shapeless cap, bearing the seal of Lady Liberty, at her. "Tuck your hair up under this. Lay down, turn your back to the door, and don't look up."

"Pretend you're asleep," Bolt advised.

"I be ten cents taller. And two shades darker."

Bolt put her hands on Fade's shoulders. "They won't be able to tell how tall you are if you're lying down. And if they don't see your face, they won't notice your color."

Coulomb grinned. "Just keep a stupid smile on your face, and they'll never know the difference."

Legion playfully hit him. Three of his other selves were on guard in the tunnels.

"Time to go," Mentaxa said. "Tserifin has opened the hatch."

"Right." Fade let herself become invisible, then ran to the Embassy. Outside the grounds, she went intangible and drifted to the basement room where Gery Allin was being held.

When she popped into being, Gery started. "Wha—?"

"Pretend I be Legion. And asleep." Fade settled on a narrow cot, turning her back to the room. She pulled the cap low over her head, and waited.

❖

The Ambassador was glad to see Tserifin. After exchanging recognition signals, the man put his arm around Tserifin's shoulders and led him up the stairs.

"It's a relief to see you, Cremen. I trust you had no trouble getting here?"

"None," Tserifin answered gruffly. "Where is the... merchandise?"

"In the safe in my office. I'll be happy to be rid of that thing, I tell you." The Ambassador frowned. "Are you sure you won't have any problem getting it offplanet?"

Tserifin stopped, shrugged off the man's arm, and stared coldly at him. "Sir, I am a professional. If the government had any doubts about my ability, I assume I would not have been given this job."

"Of course, of course," the Ambassador said nervously. "Come, I'll show you the way to my office."

As they walked, Tserifin decided to follow up his temporary advantage. "I am told that you have hostages."

"Yes. An Earth Police Cadet and another Earth teenager who violated the Embassy's grounds." The Ambassador smiled. "Officially, both are in protective custody until the EP's clear away that rabble outside."

"And unofficially?"

"Frankly, they are a headache. An embarrassment. The Police Cadet, at least, is an official of the Earth government. The teenager is a civilian. It's only a matter of time before the EP's get authority to come in and investigate."

"Hmm." Tserifin stroked his chin. "I may require one of them for safe passage. After I am gone, I suppose you can release the other without embarrassment to Chilpan."

The Ambassador's head bobbed eagerly up and down. "If you can rid me of the Police boy and the Jewel, I will be forever in your debt."

"Sir, you are in my debt now."

"Quite so." Guards stood aside, and the Ambassador let Tserifin into his office. As the Ambassador led the way to an ostentatious safe in the corner, his gaze rested for a moment on his desk. He half-turned, frowning, and Tserifin tensed. Did the man have some memory of Mentaxa's mental probes? But no, the Ambassador shook his head and continued on to the safe.

Putting one hand flat against the surface, he tapped on a keypad with the other. Then, still frowning. he looked back over his shoulder at Tserifin and said, "I haven't had anything but official dispatches from Chilpan for weeks. Tell me, how are the Wallabies doing this season?"

Tserifin's guts tightened. What the karg were the Wallabies? An athletic team? Beloved zoo animals? Flavorful fruits? Could he pretend ignorance, or were the Wallabies something that every educated Chilpani would know about? How could he possibly bluff his way out of this one?

The Ambassador's finger was still poised over the keypad, his face expectant, and Tserifin knew that he would never complete the code unless Tserifin gave a satisfactory answer.

So how *were* the Wallabies doing this season?

Tserifin rolled his eyes and tried to sound disgusted. "Please! Don't talk to me about the Wallabies! It's all one hears nowadays. I am sick to death of the whole subject."

To his relief, the Ambassador seemed to accept his bluff. He finished tapping in the code, then opened the safe and brought out a small box. "Here it is," he announced.

At a touch, the box opened to reveal a round jewel about three centimeters across. Achingly beautiful swirls of blue and white danced a stately gavotte along its surface.

"How do you intend to carry it?" the Ambassador asked.

"That is my concern," Tserifin answered, hoping he had the correct haughty tone. He held out a hand, and after a moment the Ambassador gave him the Jewel.

The Nucleus Jewel seemed almost to vibrate with an inner pulse, to quiver like a creature alive. Was it, as Tserifin had heard, a repository of all the knowledge of a long-dead race? What secrets were locked in the complex lattice of this gem— what scientific breakthroughs, what forgotten histories, what great masterpieces unseen for ten thousand generations?

Tserifin's people had lost nearly all of their own history and culture in a terrible, planet-wide war over a thousand years ago. The tragedy of that immense loss, a tragedy that dwarfed the destruction of Earth's Library of Alexandria, haunted Tserifin's society. It nearly brought tears to his eyes, to think that he—Tserifin—might have a hand in sparing another civilization such a grievous loss.

Tserifin turned his back to the Ambassador and, cradling the Nucleus Jewel in his hand, opened a pocket in the substance of his midriff. He placed the Jewel inside, then closed the pocket around it. The Jewel hummed within him.

He turned back to the Ambassador and said, "And now that hostage."

"Quite so."

They took a trip to the basement, where a guard unlocked the room that held Gery and Fade. Fade was curled up on a couch, her back to the doorway, apparently asleep; Tserifin had to admit that her disguise as Legion was effective.

Gery sat on the floor in a corner, hugging his knees. He looked up when the door opened, then lowered his head again.

"Stand up, boy," the Ambassador ordered.

Gery defiantly met the man's eyes. "Says who?"

"Don't be a fool, young man," Tserifin said. "You're to come with me."

"Make me."

Tserifin rolled his eyes. Macho bluster was the very last thing they needed now. He faced Gery squarely and said, "You will accompany me. You may do that awake and on your own two feet, or you may do it sedated and over my shoulder. Either choice is acceptable. Which will it be, please?"

Grumbling under his breath, Gery stood up.

The Ambassador gestured to Fade. "What about him?"

"Give me one hour, then release him. You may want to offer him some of your discretionary funds to avoid publicity." Inside, Tserifin smiled. In ten minutes, Fade would be gone. By then, it would be too late for the Chilpani to do anything.

"You're going now?"

"The sooner the better," Tserifin answered.

The Ambassador escorted him and Gery to the sub-basement and the tunnel behind the fusion reactor. He took hands with Tserifin. "I will report that you are on your way. When should I tell the government to expect you?"

"When I arrive," Tserifin answered. Pushing Gery before him, he entered the tunnel and sealed the hatch behind him.

The tunnel was dimly lit by a series of softly-glowing rectangles on the walls, one every three meters or so. Tserifin took Gery by the elbow and started walking.

Gery resisted.

"Grip, Gery Allin!" Tserifin whispered. "Tserifin means you no harm."

"Tserifin?"

"Quiet, please. Come with me." Still holding Gery's elbow, Tserifin broke into a trot. Gery kept pace with him.

"How…I mean, what's going on here?"

"Tserifin came to rescue you. And to retrieve the Nucleus Jewel. The PsiScouts are waiting for us where this tunnel meets the trunk line."

"I can't believe it."

"Please, we must hurry. Tserifin does not know how much longer his ruse will last." The tunnel seemed endless. Tserifin wished he could turn into a bird, or a fast-running mountain-cat—anything to get away from the Embassy quicker. But he had to stay with Gery.

The tunnel turned, was joined by another, then another at right angles. All the time, the floor sloped downward. There was a musty smell in the air, and a distant scent like stagnant water.

Another curve, and up ahead Tserifin saw the tunnel broaden, opening into a much larger space. Freedom!

"Stop!" The cry came from behind, and Tserifin spun to see the Chilpan Ambassador, flanked by four armed guards.

"Run, Gery!" But it was too late; a metal gate slammed shut across the passageway. Tserifin skidded to a halt so quickly that Gery stumbled and crashed into the gate. The thick bars did not move at all.

The Ambassador, panting, held up a hand. Four wicked rifles were trained on Tserifin and Gery. "Now," the Ambassador said, "Whoever you are, give me back the Nucleus Jewel."

Tserifin. The voice in his mind was a mere whisper, but he knew at once it came from Mentaxa. *We are right beyond the gate. Bolt is going to try to shock them—*

Tserifin shook his head. *No,* he thought firmly. *Gery is unprotected. Their guns will kill him.*

Then what do you suggest?

"I am waiting," the Ambassador said. "I will count to five, and then my guards will fire and we will have the Jewel anyway."

Tserifin doesn't know. He needs to think.

"One."

Gery touched Tserifin's arm. *Gery wants to know if you can create a diversion,* Mentaxa relayed.

Yes. Tserifin can do that.

"Two."

On four, then.

"Three. Four."

Tserifin leapt, transforming in mid-leap. His substance spread, thinned, took on the sheen of silvered glass....

On a tour of Earth's historic wonders, Tserifin had once seen the famed Hubble Space Telescope which had discovered the first habitable planets around other stars. He remembered the Hubble's polished mirror, a reflector so perfect that it seemed to have no surface of its own, just a hole into a reversed image of the room around it.

Tserifin now transformed into a duplicate of that mirror—a mirror aimed back at the Ambassador and his guards.

A gun fired, and Tserifin felt searing pain.

❖

Warned by Mentaxa, Bolt lunged forward, hands sparking like the world's most powerful arc-welder. If she had to, she'd burn through those bars.

It wasn't necessary, however. Two booted feet, each the size of a full-grown collie dog, came crashing through the gate. Gery Allin, his giant body filling the tunnel, squirmed through and pulled a great mirror after him.

Bolt felt her suit go rigid for an instant, then hurled her prepared thunderbolt down the tunnel. Coulomb was right next to her, and by the time the Chilpani guards recovered from their shock, their guns had flown from their hands.

The Ambassador turned to run, but a hand the size of a cow reached past Bolt and snagged him by the leg. Gery dragged the man, kicking and protesting, into the main tunnel.

Bolt looked back at the large mirror, which was slowly melting into a more humanoid form. Legion knelt at its side, med-kit handy. "How is he?" Bolt demanded.

Mentaxa, her gaze still glassy in deep concentration, answered tonelessly, "He'll be okay. He reflected most of the beam back at them. A few superficial burns, that's all."

The Ambassador struggled to his feet. "You have no right to trespass on sovereign Chilpani territory—"

Bolt smiled. "Your Excellency, please notice that you are standing in a public maintenance tunnel sixty meters beyond the Embassy's boundaries." She gestured. "Jav, are you getting all this?"

Jav stepped out of the shadows, grinning like a fool. Two drone pickups floated before him. "Every byte, Bolt."

Ignoring the sputtering Ambassador, Bolt held her hand out to Tserifin, who was now in his natural form. "Tserifin, may I have the Nucleus Jewel?"

The shapeshifter apparently pulled the Jewel from his navel, and handed it to Bolt. "Safe and sound, Tserifin hopes," he said.

Bolt called past Jav, "Officer Ran?"

Officer Ki Ran came forward, pushing his way past Mentaxa and Legion. His frown said at once that he was unaccustomed to traipsing around in the sewers and maintenance tunnels.

Bolt held out the Jewel. "Will you see that this is returned to the Smithsonian?"

The Ambassador stormed forward. "Officer, I demand that you arrest these...hoodlums."

Ran turned eyes of ice on the Ambassador. "On what grounds?"

"They...trespassing, for one. Assault on a diplomatic personage. Theft of property that belongs to the Chilpan Cluster Government."

"Oh," Bolt said, sweetly, "Then you admit that the Chilpan Government was in possession of the stolen Nucleus Jewel?"

"I...we..." He snorted. "The Chilpan Government admits nothing."

Officer Ran leaned forward. "Do you still want these hoodlums arrested?"

The man quivered in rage. "No! I want nothing at all to do with them. Ever!" He limped toward the tunnel, crawling over the broken gates.

Bolt couldn't resist needling further. "His Excellency seems to have gotten lost in the tunnels. Does he need an escort back to the Embassy?"

"Get out of my sight. All of you." He turned to Bolt, his eyes burning. "And pray you never find yourself in the Chilpan Cluster. Any of you." With that, he spun and waddled off down the tunnel.

"We'll do our best," Bolt replied, laughing.

❖

EARTHNET alt.trends.commentary ON Wed Apr 27, 2574 Sec: 1
Conf: 1
{RTC RECEIVE ONLY}
[RUNNING ARCHIVE TO Sec: 1 Thread: 307] ** RESPOND ON
Sec: 1 Conf: 4 **
FROM: NETJAY [Jav Man] AT 12:41:23
———————————

[THIS IS A REALTIME REPORT]
Welcome, netheads and PsiScouts fans, to PsiScouts
Plaza, here in the shadow of the Lady Named Liberty on this
bright and beautiful spring day. As you can see, the
assembled Movers and Shakers of the planet are gathered
here to pay tribute to the PsiScouts. We knew you'd come
around, latelings, to our point of view. These are kids who can
Do No Wrong.

Now, I can't confirm or deny the particulars of the Scouts'
latest case, and I'm sure you're as tired of the rumors as I am.
[REF: Key 3364 for link to alt.gossip.diplo] But I can confirm the
happy news that the Earth Police have gotten over their little
spat with the Scouts, as this afternoon's ceremony will make
abundantly clear.

First, however, the PsiScouts have some unfinished
business of their own. For that, I am proud to bring you The
PsiScouts: Bolt, Mentaxa, Coulomb, and Fade!
———————————

❖

Coulomb felt shy in front of all these faces—the President
of Earth, Mayor Hua, King Philip, De' Artveldt, a thousand
others. Almost every gang on Earth, it seemed, had sent
representatives...all of them in Youth Corps colors. And the
Irregulars were out in full force, too.

For an instant, it was all too much. Coulomb wanted to
run, to go back inside HQ and hide in his room. But Mentaxa
beside him, Bolt's exultation echoing in his mind, and Fade's
quiet certainty calmed him.

"Gentlefolk of the Galaxy," Bolt said, her words booming
across the crowded plaza and resounding in living rooms

throughout the Myriad Worlds, "It is my pleasure to welcome these three new recruits to our ranks. They are everything that the Youth Corps and the PsiScouts stand for: kids who are brave, intelligent, responsible. Kids who take a stand, and aren't afraid to do what needs to be done. You should be proud of them."

Coulomb shivered. And it wasn't the chill breeze.

"Last week these kids were ordinary teenagers, lost in a world they hadn't made. Now they're PsiScouts. Last week, they were Lethim and Tserifin and Gery. Now…" she hesitated, and Coulomb saw the glint of a tear in her eye, "Now, I give you the newest PsiScouts:

"Legion."

Six Lethims stepped forward, then merged and waved at the cheering crowd.

"Mimic."

Tserifin, a giant eagle, swooped down from the sky—and transformed into himself, a grey-skinned creature with wide eyes, stubby tail, and a PsiScouts uniform of green and black.

"And Colossus."

In seven-league boots and a crimson uniform, Gery emerged from behind Lady Liberty, gave her a bow, and then shrunk down to the size of a normal kid.

The crowd went wild.

It took Bolt more than a few minutes to hush them. The 'dults were worse than the kids. Finally, though, she had them as quiet as they were likely to be. "Now, I'd like to introduce our mentor, our inspiration, the woman who started the PsiScouts: Colleen Artveldt."

De' Artveldt took Bolt's position. Wind whipped her hair, and there was more than a trace of tears in her eyes. "I can't say anything about the Scouts that speaks louder than their own actions." She surveyed them all. "Children, you have a right to be proud. And we have a right to be proud of you." She smiled at the PsiScouts. "I hope you'll forgive an old lady her sentimentality. I know this was supposed to be a simple ceremony to announce the new Scouts…but this seems as good a time as any. Chief?"

Earth Police Chief Ormandeau waddled to De' Artveldt's side, looking very uncomfortable. "I'm not accustomed to public speaking," he said, "So I'll make this quick. Step forward as I say your name. Bolt. Mentaxa."

What is he up to?

"Coulomb. Fade."

I have no idea.

"Legion. Mimic. Colossus."

It could be anything, with Colleen involved. Look at her grin.

"By virtue of my authority as Chief of the Earth Police, and as an officer in the Interstellar Police Force, I hereby deputize these individuals as fully-empowered law enforcement officers under the Olympus Convention. On any planet of the Myriad Worlds, the PsiScouts are authorized to make arrests. I request that they receive the full co-operation of local law forces. And may I say, I for one will sleep better knowing these kids are on the job."

This time, the applause was deafening. But Coulomb didn't really mind.

❖

Appendix:
The PsiScouts

Bolt (Gael Rimma of Wargal): Age 15. Bolt's psi powers give her limited control of electrical fields, plus the ability to generate spontaneous electrical currents.

Colossus (Gery Allin of Earth): Age 16. Colossus is able to increase his size and strength at will.

Coulomb (Royd Kar of Taarla): Age 14. Coulomb is a telekinetic with the ability to manipulate the magnetic fields and forces around him.

Fade (Tovi Witzell of Tyzgab): Age 14. Fade can render herself partially or completely invisible and intangible.

Legion (Lethim Barog of Garagk): Age 13. Legion can manifest up to six simultaneous astral bodies, each as apparently solid as his own.

Mentaxa (Iris Krall of Ceres): Age 15. Mentaxa is a powerful and accomplished telepath.

Mimic (Kheen Kharrn of Nortlin): Age 14. Mimic is a shapeshifter, able to take on the shape of any object or creature.

The Scattered Worlds Mosaic by Don Sakers

Dance for the Ivory Madonna
a romance of psiberspace
Print & Kindle
Spectrum Award finalist; 56 Hugo nominations
*"Imagine a Stand on Zanzibar written by a left-wing Robert Heinlein, and infused with the most exciting possibilities of the new cyber-technology." -Melissa Scott,
author of Dreaming Metal, The Jazz*

Weaving the Web of Days
a tale of the Scattered Worlds
Print & Kindle
Maj Thovold has led the Galaxy for three decades, a Golden Age of peace and prosperity. She is weary and ready to resign, but she faces one last battle: a battle on the strangest battlefield known: a web of living tendrils that stretches across interstellar space. A web where Maj's enemies wait, like spiders, for their prey....

The Eighth Succession
a novel of the Scattered Worlds
Print & Kindle
"Remember when science fiction used to be filled with galactic intrigue and bigger-than-life heroes? The wonderful Don Sakers certainly does! The Eighth Succession is a rip-roaring yarn, impossible to put down. If John W. Campbell's Astounding Stories had been published in an LGBT-friendly era, this is the cover-story serial you'd have been waiting anxiously for each month. What a ride!" -Robert J. Sawyer, Hugo Award-winning author of Red Planet Blues

Children of the Eighth Day
a novel of the Scattered Worlds
Print & Kindle
The Eighth Succession *introduced readers to the Hoister Family...* Children of the Eighth Day *takes the story of this remarkable family to the exciting next level.*

The Scattered Worlds Mosaic by Don Sakers

All Roads Lead to Terra

two tales of the Scattered Worlds

Kindle only

Two exciting tales tell of attacks against the shining jewel of the Terran Empire: Earth. Includes an introduction and notes from the author.

A Voice in Every Wind

two tales of the Scattered Worlds

Print & Kindle

On a world where meaning lives in every rock and stream, and every breeze brings a new voice, one human explorer stands on the threshold of discoveries that could alter the future of Humanity.

A Rose From Old Terra

a novel of the Scattered Worlds

Print & Kindle

Jedrek left the Grand Library and his work circle eleven years ago. Now a crisis in uncharted space brings the circle back together. Soon, Jedrek and his friends are at the focal point of a clash of cultures, and the only thing that can save the Galaxy is one modest group of Librarians.

The Leaves of October

a novel of the Scattered Worlds

Print & Kindle

Compton Crook Award finalist

The Hlutr: Immensely old, terribly wise…and utterly alien. When mankind went out into the stars, he found the Hlutr waiting for him. Waiting to observe, to converse, to help. Waiting to judge…and, if necessary, to destroy.

More Books from Speed-of-C Productions

The Curse of the Zwilling by Don Sakers
Print & Kindle

It's Hogwarts meets Buffy at Patapsco University: a small, cozy liberal arts college like so many others – except for the Department of Comparative Religion, where age-old spells are taught and magic is practiced. When a favorite teacher is found dead under mysterious circumstances, grad student David Galvin finds that a malevolent evil has awakened. And now David, along with four novice undergrads, must defeat this ancient, malignant terror.

The SF Book of Days by Don Sakers
Print only

Drawn from the pages of classic sf literature, here is a science fiction/fantasy event for every day of the year…and for quite a few days that aren't *part of the year. From Doc Brown's arrival in Hill Valley (January 1, 1885) to the launch of the* Bellerophon *(Sextor 7, 2351), this datebook is truly out of this world.*

PsiScouts #2: Bright Promise by Don Sakers & Phil Meade
Print & Kindle

In the 26th century, psi-powered teenagers from all over the Myriad Worlds join together as the heroic PsiScouts. Whether it's a mission deep into a theocracy to rescue endangered kids, or a time-travel odyssey to save history itself, the PsiScouts are equal to the challenge.

Meat and Machine: queer writings by Don Sakers
Print & Kindle

Don Sakers has been queering sf and fantasy for three decades. Meat and Machine collects 24 short pieces of Don's science fiction, fantasy, nonfiction, and erotics.

Elevenses by Don Sakers
Print & Kindle

Eleven SF and fantasy short stories intended as bite-size snacks.

More Books from Speed-of-C Productions

Gaylaxicon Sampler 2006
Print only

Sample the work of thirteen writers from across the spectrum of gay, lesbian, bisexual, and/or transgender science fiction, fantasy, and/or horror. Includes big names and small, much-published veterans and promising beginners, Lammy and Spectrum Award nominees and winners, past Gaylaxicon Guests of Honor, and fresh new names.

QSpec Sampler 2007
Print only

Originally prepared as a giveaway at Gaylaxicon 2007 in Atlanta, this volume is available at a nominal charge as a sampler of the fine work being done by GLBT writers in SF, fantasy, and horror.

Act Well Your Part by Don Sakers
Print & Kindle

A beloved gay young adult romance, back in print for its adult fans as well as a new generation of teens. At first Keith Graff dislikes his new school. He misses his old friends, and despairs of ever fitting in. Then he joins the school's drama club, and meets the boyishly cute Bran Davenport....

Lucky in Love by Don Sakers
Print & Kindle

A companion novel to Act Well Your Part, Lucky in Love *follows Keith's friend Frank, torn between bad boy Dwight and basketball star Darnell.*

A Cosmos of Many Mansions: Varieties of SF by Don Sakers
Print & Kindle

Based on the first five years of Sakers's popular review column, this volume examines & explains dozens of types of science fiction along with hundreds of reviews.

The Mud of the Place by Susanna J. Sturgis
Print only

"A sensitive, witty, and tightly plotted portrayal of life on Martha's Vineyard that only a true Islander could have written. Nice going, Susanna!" –Cynthia Riggs